JOHN CREASEY'S
CRIME COLLECTION 1978

JOHN CREASEY'S CRIME COLLECTION 1978

An Anthology by members of the Crime Writers' Association

edited by

HERBERT HARRIS

LONDON
VICTOR GOLLANCZ LTD
1978

ISBN 0 575 02500 X

MADE AND PRINTED IN GREAT BRITAIN BY
THE GARDEN CITY PRESS LIMITED
LETCHWORTH, HERTFORDSHIRE
SG6 1JS

CONTENTS

Eric Ambler: The Blood Bargain 9

Joan Aiken: The Companion 25

Kenneth Benton: Gifted Amateurs 34

Michael Gilbert: The Decline and Fall of Mr Behrens 57

Miriam Sharman: The Annex 73

H. R. F. Keating: Mrs Craggs and the Lords Spiritual and Temporal 88

Peter Godfrey: The Newtonian Egg 99

Herbert Harris: The Big Fix 113

Julian Symons: The Woman Afraid of October 120

Margaret Yorke: Always Rather a Prig 131

Jeffry Scott: "What You Gain on the Swings . . ." 140

Penelope Wallace: Tell David 148

James Pattinson: Murder in Mind 159

Judy Chard: Scent of Lilac 165

John Rossiter: "Yes, Sir: No, Sir" 170

ACKNOWLEDGEMENTS

To *Winter's Crimes 2* (Macmillan 1970) for "The Blood Bargain" by Eric Ambler; to *International Storyteller* for "Scent of Lilac" by Judy Chard; to *Argosy* for "The Decline and Fall of Mr Behrens" by Michael Gilbert; to *Ellery Queen's Mystery Magazine* for "The Newtonian Egg" by Peter Godfrey; to the *Mike Shayne Mystery Magazine* for "The Big Fix" by Herbert Harris; to the BBC's "Morning Story" (1966) for "Murder in Mind" by James Pattinson; to *Alfred Hitchcock's Mystery Magazine* for "The Annex" by Miriam Sharman; to *Francis Quarles Investigates* (Panther Books 1965) for "The Woman Afraid of October" by Julian Symons; to the *Edgar Wallace Mystery Magazine* for "Tell David" by Penelope Wallace; and to Joan Aiken, Kenneth Benton, H. R. F. Keating, John Rossiter, Jeffry Scott and Margaret Yorke for original contributions.

INTRODUCTION

ONE DAY IN November 1953—appropriately enough, Guy Fawkes Day—the late John Creasey summoned together at the National Liberal Club in London what might be called a coven of crime writers, fourteen in number, and suggested that they form themselves into an Association.

Thus the Crime Writers' Association was born, and this year, with four hundred members and an international flavour, it is celebrating its Silver Jubilee. *John Creasey's Crime Collection 1978* therefore coincides with the C.W.A.'s twenty-fifth anniversary, and it is interesting to note that two of the authors in this collection, Michael Gilbert and Julian Symons, were among the original fourteen founder-members.

As Honorary Editor of a dozen C.W.A. anthologies, I have been asked why John Creasey's name is still linked with this annual collection of stories, since he died six years ago. The answer is quite simple. In 1960 Creasey founded his annual *John Creasey's Mystery Bedside Book*, and after editing six editions he made over the title to the C.W.A. in 1966 for use as their own anthology, the bulk of the royalties to go into the Association's funds. I was entrusted with the task of ensuring its continuity. I compiled a further ten editions under the original title, but in 1977, when it appeared for the first time under the Gollancz imprint, it was decided to call it *John Creasey's Crime Collection*, still retaining the name of the Association's founder. Earnings from the book continue to support C.W.A. funds.

Of the authors in this volume, four—Kenneth Benton, H. R. F. Keating, Julian Symons and myself—have served as Chairman of the Association; and four—Eric Ambler, H. R. F. Keating, Julian Symons, and the writer of these notes—have received C.W.A. "Dagger" Awards. Readers may also like to know that Penelope Wallace, contributing to this collection, is the daughter of the immortal Edgar, and that Margaret Yorke is currently serving as the C.W.A. Vice-Chairman.

HERBERT HARRIS

THE BLOOD BARGAIN

Eric Ambler

Ex-President Fuentes enjoys a peculiar distinction. More people would like to kill him now that he is in retirement than wanted to kill him when he was in power.

He is a puzzled and indignant man.

What he fails to understand is that, while men like General Perez may in time forgive you for robbing them, they will never forgive you for making them look foolish.

The *coup d'état* which overthrew Fuentes' Social Action Party government was well organised and relatively bloodless.

The leaders of the *coup* were mostly Army officers, but they had understandings with fellow dissidents in the Air Force and Navy as well as the discreet blessing of the Church. A price for the collaboration of the Chief of Police had been agreed upon well in advance, and the lists of certain left-wing deputies, militant trade union officials, pro-government newspaper editors, Castro-trained subversives and other undesirables whose prompt arrest would be advisable, had been compiled with his help. Similar arrangements had been made in the larger provincial towns. Although the conspirators were by no means all of the same political complexion, they had for once found themselves able to sink their differences in the pursuit of a common goal. Whatever might come afterwards, they were all agreed upon one thing; if the country were to be saved from corruption, Communist subversion, anarchy, bankruptcy, civil war and, ultimately, foreign military intervention, President Fuentes had to go.

One evening in September he went.

The tactics employed by the "Liberation Front" conspirators followed the pattern which has become more or less traditional when a *coup* is backed by organised military forces and opposed, if it is opposed at all, only by civilian mobs and confused, lightly armed garrison units.

As darkness fell, the tanks of two armoured brigades together with trucks containing a parachute regiment, signals units and a company of combat engineers rolled into the capital. Within little more than an hour, they had secured their major objectives. Meanwhile, the Air Force had taken over the international airport, grounded all planes and established a headquarters in the customs and immigration building. An infantry division now began to move into the city and take up positions which would enable it to deal with the civil disturbances which were expected to develop as news of the *coup*, and of the mass arrests which were accompanying it, reached the densely populated slum areas with their high concentrations of Fuentes supporters.

A little after eight-thirty a squadron of tanks and a special task force of paratroopers reached the Presidential Palace. The Palace guard resisted for a quarter of an hour and suffered casualties of eight wounded. The order to surrender was given personally to the guard commander by President Fuentes "in order to avoid further bloodshed."

When this was reported to General Perez, the leader of the *coup*, he drove to the Palace. He was accompanied by five senior members of the Liberation Front council, including the Chief of Police, and no less than three representatives of the foreign press. The latter had been flushed out of the Jockey Club bar by an aide earlier in the evening and hastily briefed on the aims and ideals of the Liberation Front. General Perez wished to lose no time in establishing himself abroad as a magnanimous, reasonable and responsible man, and his regime as worthy of prompt diplomatic recognition.

The newsmen's accounts of the interview between President Fuentes and General Perez, and of the now-notorious "blood bargain" which emerged from it, were all in substantial agreement. At the time the bargain seemed to them just another of those civilised, oddly chivalrous agreements to live and let live which, by testifying to the continued presence of compassion and good sense even at moments of turmoil and destruction, have so often lightened the long, dark history of Latin American revolution. The reporters, all experienced men, can scarcely be blamed for misunderstanding it. They knew, as everyone else knew, that President Fuentes was a devious and deeply dishonest man. The only mistake they made was in assuming that the other parties to the bargain had made due allowance for that deviousness and dishonesty and knew exactly what they were doing. What the reporters had not realised was that these normally wary and hard-headed officers had become so intoxicated by the speed and extent of their initial success, that by the time they reached the Presidential Palace they were no longer capable of thinking clearly.

President Fuentes received General Perez and the other Liberation Front leaders in the ornate Cabinet Room of the Palace to which he had been taken by the paratroopers who had arrested him. With him were the other male occupants of the Presidential air raid shelter at the time of his arrest. These included the Palace guard commander, the President's valet, the Palace majordomo, two footmen and the man who looked after the Palace plumbing system, in addition to the Minister of Public Welfare, the Minister of Agrarian Education, the Minister of Justice and the elderly Controller of the Presidential Secretariat. The Minister of Public Welfare had brought a bottle of brandy with him from the shelter and smiled glassily throughout the subsequent confrontation. Agrarian Education and Justice maintained expressions of bewilderment and indignation, but confined their oral protests to circumspect murmurs. The thin-lipped young captain in charge of the paratroopers handled his machine pistol as if he would have been glad of an excuse to use it.

Only the President seemed at ease. There was even a touch of impatience in the shrug with which he rose to face General Perez and his party as they strode in from the anteroom; it was as if he had been interrupted by some importunate visitor during a game of bridge.

His calm was only partly assumed. He knew all about General Perez' sensitivity to foreign opinion, and he had immediately recognised the newsmen in the rear of the procession. They would not have been brought there if any immediate violence to his person had been contemplated.

The impatience he displayed was certainly genuine; it was impatience with himself. He had known for weeks that a *coup* was in preparation, and had taken the precaution a month earlier of sending his wife and children and his mistress out of the country. They were all now in Washington, and he had planned, using as a pretext his announced wish to address personally a meeting of the Organisation of American States, to join them there the following week. His private spies had reported that the *coup* would undoubtedly be timed to take advantage of his absence abroad. Since the *coup* by means of which he himself had come to power five years earlier had been timed in that way, he had been disposed to believe the report.

Now, he knew better. Whether or not his spies had deliberately deceived him did not matter at the moment. A mistake had been made which was, he knew, likely to cost him more than temporary inconvenience. Unless he could retrieve it immediately, by getting out of the country within the next few hours, that mistake would certainly cost him his liberty, and most probably his life, too.

He had risked death before, was familiar with the physical and mental sensations that accompanied the experience, and with a small effort was able to ignore them. As General Perez came up to him, the President displayed no emotion of any kind. He merely nodded politely and waited for the General to speak.

For a moment the General seemed tongue-tied. He was sweating too. As this was the first time he had overthrown a government he was undoubtedly suffering from stage fright. He took refuge finally in military punctilio. With a click of the heels he came to attention and fixed his eyes on the President's left ear.

"We are here . . ." he began harshly, then cleared his throat and corrected himself. "I and my fellow members of the Council of the Liberation Front are here to inform you that a state of national emergency now exists."

The President nodded politely. "I am glad to have that information, General. Since telephone communication has been cut off I have naturally been curious as to what was happening. These gentlemen"—he motioned to the paratroopers—"seemed unwilling to enlighten me."

The General ignored this and went on as if he were reading a proclamation. In fact, he was quoting from the press release which had already been handed to the newsmen. "Directed by the Council and under its orders," he said, "the armed forces have assumed control of all functions of civil government in the state, and, as provided in the Constitution, formally demand your resignation."

The President looked astounded. "You have the effrontery to claim constitutional justification for this mutiny?"

For the first time since he had entered the room the General relaxed slightly. "We have a precedent, sir. Nobody should know that better than you. You yourself set it when you legalised your own seizure of power from your predecessor. Need I remind you of the wording of the amendment? 'If for any reason, including the inability to fulfil the duties of his office by reason of ill-health, mental or physical, or absence, an elected president is unable to exercise the authority vested in him under the constitution, a committee representative of the nation and those responsible to it for the maintenance of law and order may request his resignation and be entitled. . . .' "

For several seconds the President had been waving his hands for silence. Now he broke in angrily. "Yes, yes, I know all about that. But my predecessor was absent. I am not. Neither am I ill, physically or mentally. There are no legal grounds on which you are entitled to ask for my resignation."

"No legal grounds, sir?" General Perez could smile now. He pointed to the paratroopers. "Are you able to exercise the authority of a president? *Are* you? If you think so, try."

The President pretended to think over the challenge. The interview was so far going more or less as he had expected; but the next moves would be the critical ones for him. He walked over to a window and back in order to give himself time to collect himself.

Everyone there was watching him. The tension in the room

was mounting. He could feel it. It was odd, he thought. Here he was, a prisoner, wholly at their mercy; and yet they were waiting for him to come to a decision, to make a choice where no choice existed. It was absurd. All they wanted from him was relief from a small and quite irrational sense of guilt. They had the Church's blessings; now the poor fools yearned for the blessing of the law, too. Very well. They should have it. But it would be expensive.

He turned and faced General Perez again.

"A resignation exacted from me under duress would have no force in law," he said.

The General glanced at the Chief of Police. "You are a lawyer, Raymundo. Who represents the law here?"

"The Council of the Liberation Front, General."

Perez looked at the President again. "You see, sir, there are no technical difficulties. We even have the necessary document already prepared."

His aide held up a black leather portfolio.

The President hesitated, looking from one face to another as if hoping against hope that he might find a friendly one. Finally he shrugged. "I will read the document," he said coldly and walked towards the cabinet table. As he did so he seemed to become aware again of his fellow prisoners in the room. He stopped suddenly.

"Must my humiliation be witnessed by my colleagues and my servants as well as the foreign press?" he demanded bitterly.

General Perez motioned to the paratrooper captain. "Take those men into another room. Leave guards outside the doors of this one."

The President waited until the group from the air raid shelter had been herded out, then sat down at the table. The General's aide opened the portfolio, took out a legal document laced with green ribbon and placed it in front of the President.

He made a show of studying the document very carefully. In fact, he was indifferent to its contents. His intention was simply to let the tension mount a little further and to allow the other men there to feel that they were on the point of getting what they wanted.

For three minutes there was dead silence in the room. It was broken only by the sound of distant machine-gun fire. It seemed to be coming from the south side of the city. The President heard a slight stir from the group of men behind him and one of them cleared his throat nervously. There was another burst of firing. The President took no notice of it. He read the document through a third time then put it down and sat back in his chair.

The aide offered him a pen with which to sign. The President ignored it and turned his head so that he could see General Perez.

"You spoke of a resignation, General," he said. "You did not mention that it was to be a confession also."

"Hardly a confession, sir," the General replied drily. "We would not expect you voluntarily to incriminate yourself. The admission is only of incompetence. That is not yet a criminal offence in a head of state."

The President smiled faintly. "And if I were to sign this paper, what kind of personal treatment might I expect to receive afterwards? A prison cell perhaps, with a carefully staged treason trial to follow? Or merely a bullet in the head and an unmarked grave?"

The General reddened. "We are here to correct abuses of power, sir, not to imitate them. When you have signed you will be conducted to your former home in Alazan province. You will be expected to remain there for the present and the Governor of the province will be instructed to see that you do so. Apart from that restriction you will be free to do as you please. Your family will naturally be permitted to join you."

"You mention the house in Alazan province. What about my other personal property?"

"You will be permitted to retain everything you owned when you took office."

"I see." The President stood up and moved away from the table. "I will think about it. I will let you have my decision tomorrow," he added casually.

The silence that followed this announcement did not last long, but one of the newsmen reported later that it was one of the loudest he had ever heard. Another remembered that during it he suddenly became conscious of the presence and smell of a large bowl of tropical flowers on a side table by the anteroom door.

The President had walked towards the windows again. General Perez took two steps towards him, then stopped.

"You must decide at once! You must sign now!" he snapped.

The President turned on him. "Why? Why now?"

It was the Chief of Police who answered him. "Son of a whore, because we tell you to!" he shouted.

Suddenly they were all shouting at him. One officer was so enraged that he drew his pistol. The General had difficulty in restoring order.

The President took no notice of them. He kept his eyes on General Perez, but it was really the newsmen he was addressing now. As the din subsided he raised his voice.

"I asked a question, General. Why now? Why the haste? It is a reasonable question. If, as you say, you already control the country, what have you to fear from me? Or is it, perhaps, that your control is not in fact as complete and effective as you would have us believe?"

The General had to quell another angry outburst from his colleagues before he could answer, but he preserved his own temper admirably. His reply was calm and deliberate.

"I will tell you exactly what we control so that you may judge for yourself," he said. "To begin with all provincial army garrisons, air force establishments and police posts have declared for the Liberation Front, as have five out of eight of the provincial governors. The three objectors—I am sure you will have guessed who they are—have been rendered harmless and replaced by military governors. None of this can come as a great surprise to you I imagine. You never had much support outside the capital and the mining areas."

The President nodded. "Stupidity can sometimes be charted geographically," he remarked.

"Now as to the capital. We control the airfields, both military and civil, the naval base, all communications including telephone and radio and television broadcast facilities, the power stations, all fuel oil storage facilities, all main traffic arteries, all government offices and city police posts together with the offices and printing presses of *El Correo* and *La Gaceta*." He glanced at his watch. "In connection with the broadcast facilities, I may mention that while the television station is temporarily off the air, the radio station will shortly begin broadcasting an announcement of the establishment of the new Liberation Front regime, which I recorded two days ago. As I told you before, everything is now under our control."

The President smiled and glanced significantly at the newsmen. "Are the *sumideri* under control, General?"

Sumideri, meaning sinks or drains, was the popular slang term used to describe the slum areas on the south side of the capital.

The General hesitated only an instant. "The southern area is effectively contained," he replied stiffly. "The first infantry division reinforced by the third tank brigade has that responsibility."

"I see." The President looked again at the newsmen. "So the civil war may be expected to begin at any moment."

With a quick motion of his hands the General silenced the chorus of objections from his colleagues. "We are fully prepared to deal firmly with any mob violence which may occur," he said. "Of that you may be sure."

"Yes," said the President bitterly, "perhaps civil war is not the phrase to use for the planned massacre of unarmed civilians." He swung around suddenly to face the newsmen and his voice hardened. "You have been witnesses to this farce, gentlemen. I ask you to remember it well and let the civilised world know of it. These men come to ask for my resignation as head of state. That is all they want! Why? Because outside in the streets of the city their tanks and guns are waiting to begin the slaughter of the thousands of men and women who will protest their loyalty to me. And the way to bring them out for the slaughter is to fling my resignation like so much filth in their faces!"

General Perez could stand it no longer. "That is a lie!" he shouted.

The President turned on him savagely. "Do you think they

will *not* come out? Why else are they 'contained' as you call it? Why else? Because they are my people and because they will listen only to me."

A glow of triumph suffused General Perez' angry face. "Then their blood will be on *your* hands!" he roared. He stabbed a forefinger at the newsmen. "You heard what he said, gentlemen. *They do what he tells them!* It is his responsibility, then, not ours, if they oppose us. *He* will be the murderer of women and children! Let him deny it."

This time the President made no reply. He just stood there looking about him in bewilderment, like a boxer who has staggered to his feet after a count of ten and can't quite realise that the fight is over. At last he walked slowly back to the cabinet table, sat down heavily and buried his head in his hands.

Nobody else moved. When the President raised his head and looked at them again his eyes were haggard. He spoke very quietly.

"You are right," he said; "they are my people and they will do as I tell them. It is my responsibility. I accept it. There must be no senseless bloodshed. I think it is my duty to tell them not to protest."

For a moment they all stared at him incredulously. The Chief of Police started to say something, then stopped as he caught General Perez' eye. If the man were serious this was too good an opportunity to miss.

General Perez went over and addressed the President. "I cannot believe that even you would speak lightly on such a matter, but I must ask if you seriously mean what you say."

The President nodded absently. "I will need about an hour to draft my statement. There is a direct line to the radio station here in the Palace and the necessary equipment. The station can record me on tape." He managed a rueful smile. "In the circumstances, I imagine that you would prefer a recording to a live broadcast."

"Yes." But the General was still reluctant to believe in his triumph. "How can you be sure that they will obey you," he asked.

The President thought before he answered. "There will be some, of course, who will be too distressed, too angry perhaps, to do as I ask," he said. "But if the officers commanding troops are ordered to use restraint, casualties can be kept to a minimum." He glanced at the Chief of Police. "There should be moderation, too, in respect of arrests. But the majority will listen to me, I think." He paused. "The important thing is that they must believe that I am speaking as a free man, and not out of fear because there is a pistol at my head."

"I myself can give them that assurance," said the General. The fact that he could make such an ingenuous suggestion is an indication of his mental confusion at that point.

The President raised his eyebrows. "With all respect, General, I don't think we could expect them at this time to believe you of all people. I also think that the news that I am to be kept under what amounts to house arrest in Alazan province will not help to convince them either."

"Then what do you propose? You can scarcely remain here in the capital."

"Naturally not." The President sat back in his chair. He had assumed a statesmanlike air now. "It is quite clear," he said, "that we must achieve an orderly and responsible transfer of power. I shall, of course, resign in order to make way for the Liberation Front. However, in your place, I must say that I would regard my continued presence anywhere in this country as undesirable. These people to whom I am to appeal tonight will only respond with restraint because of their loyalty to me. That loyalty will continue as long as they are able to give expression to it. You would do better really to get rid of me. As soon as I have spoken to my people you should get me out of the country as quickly as you can."

"Exile?" It was the Chief of Police who spoke up now. "But if we exile you that looks no better than house arrest in Alazan. Worse, possibly."

"Exactly." The President nodded approvingly. "The solution I suggest is that I am permitted to announce to my people that I will continue to serve them, the nation and the Liberation Front, but in a different capacity and abroad. Our embassy in

Nicaragua is without an ambassador at present. That would be a suitable appointment. I suggest that after I have recorded my broadcast I leave the country immediately in order to take up my post."

The council discussion that ensued lacked the vehemence of the earlier exchanges. The strain of the past twenty-four hours was beginning to tell on General Perez and his colleagues; they were getting tired; and the sounds of firing from the south side were becoming more insistent. Time was running out. It was one of the newsmen who drew their attention to the fact.

"General," he said to Perez, "has it occurred to you that if the President doesn't talk to these people of his pretty soon they're all going to be out on the streets anyway?"

The President recognised the urgency, too, but refused to be hurried. As he pointed out, there were matters of protocol to be dealt with before he could make his appeal to the people. For one thing, his resignation would have to be redrafted. Since, he argued, he was now to be appointed his country's ambassador to Nicaragua, references in the present draft to his incompetence would obviously have to be deleted. And there were other clauses which might be interpreted as reflections on his personal integrity.

In the end, the President wrote his own act of resignation. It was a simple document but composed with great care. His radio speech, on the other hand, he scribbled out on a cabinet desk pad while technicians, hastily summoned by jeep from the central radio building, were setting up a recording circuit in the anteroom.

Meanwhile, telephone communication had been restored to the Palace, and the Controller of the Presidential Secretariat had been released from arrest and put to work in his office.

His first task had been to contact the Nicaraguan Ambassador, give him a discreetly censored account of the current situation and request him to ascertain immediately, in accordance with Article 8 of the Pan-American Convention, if his government would be prepared to accept ex-President Fuentes as *persona grata* in the capacity of ambassador to their country.

The Nicaraguan Ambassador had undertaken to telephone personally to the Minister of Foreign Relations in Managua and report back. His unofficial opinion was that there would be no opposition to the proposed appointment.

With the help of the air force council member present the Controller next spoke to the officer in charge at the International Airport. He learned that of the two civil airliners grounded earlier that evening, one had been southbound to Caracas, the other, a Colombian Avianca jet, had been northbound to Mexico City. Fortunately, a Vice-Consul from the Colombian Consulate-General was already at the airport, having been summoned there by the Avianca captain to protest at the grounding. The Controller spoke with the Vice-Consul who said that Avianca would be willing to carry ex-President Fuentes as a passenger to Mexico City if the Mexican Government would permit him to land. A call to the Mexican Embassy explaining that ex-President Fuentes would be in transit through Mexican territory on his way to his post as an accredited diplomatic representative to the Republic of Nicaragua secured the necessary permission.

The President already had a diplomatic passport which needed only minor amendments to fit it for its new role. All that was needed now to facilitate his departure was confirmation from the Nicaraguan Ambassador that he would be accorded diplomatic status in Managua. Within an hour, the Nicaraguan Government, acting promptly in the belief that they were helping both parties to the arrangement, had replied favourably.

The escape route was open.

President Fuentes made two tape-recordings of the appeal to his supporters, one for the radio, the second for use by a loudspeaker van in the streets of the *sumideri*. Then he signed his resignation and was driven to the airport. General Perez provided an escort of armoured cars.

The plane, with ex-President Fuentes on board, took off a little after midnight. Five hours later it landed in Mexico City.

News of the Liberation Front *coup* and of the President's voluntary resignation and ambassadorial appointment had been carried by all the international wire services, and there were reporters waiting for him. There was also, despite the early hour, a protocol official from the Department of External Relations to meet him. Fuentes made a brief statement to the reporters, confirming the fact of his resignation. On the subject of his appointment as Ambassador to Nicaragua he was vague. He then drove to a hotel in the city. On the way there he asked the protocol official if it would be convenient for him to call upon the Minister of External Affairs later that day.

The official was mildly surprised. As Ambassador Fuentes was merely passing through Mexico, a brief note of thanks to the Minister would normally be the only courtesy expected of him. On the other hand, the circumstances of Fuentes' sudden translation from President to Ambassador were unusual and it was possible that the Minister might be glad of the opportunity of hearing what Fuentes himself had to say on the subject. He promised that he would consult the Minister's personal assistant at the earliest possible moment.

The Minister received Ambassador Fuentes at five o'clock that afternoon.

The two men had met before, at conferences of the Organisation of American States and on the occasion of a state visit to Mexico paid by Fuentes soon after he became President. It was a tribute to the Minister's natural courtesy as well as his self-discipline that Fuentes believed that the Minister liked him. In fact the Minister viewed him with dislike and disapproval and had not been in the least surprised or distressed by the news of the Liberation Front *coup*. However, he had been amused by Fuentes' ability to emerge from the situation not only alive and free but also invested with diplomatic immunity; and it modified his distaste for the man. He was, one had to admit, an engaging scoundrel.

After the preliminary politeness had been disposed of the Minister inquired courteously whether he could be of any service to the Ambassador during his stay in Mexico.

Fuentes inclined his head: "That is most kind of you, Mr Minister," he said graciously. "Yes, there is one thing."

"You only have to ask."

"Thank you." Ambassador Fuentes straightened up a little in

his chair. "I wish," he said, "to make formal application to be considered here as a refugee, and formally to request political asylum in the United States of Mexico."

The Minister stared for a moment, then smiled.

"Surely you must be joking, Mr Ambassador."

"Not in the least."

The Minister was puzzled, and because he was puzzled he put into words the first obvious objection that came into his head.

"But in the United States of Mexico, even though you are not accredited to the Federal Government, you already, by virtue of the Pan-American Convention, enjoy diplomatic status and privileges here," he said.

It was a statement which he was later to regret.

Ambassador Fuentes never took up his post in Nicaragua.

One of the first official acts of General Perez' Council of the Liberation Front was to set up a committee, headed by the Professor of Political Economy at Bolivar University, to report on the financial state of the Republic.

It took the committee only a few days to discover that during the past three years ex-President Fuentes had authorised printings of five hundred peseta bank-notes to a total value of one hundred million dollars and that twenty of those hundred millions could not be accounted for.

The Governor of the National Bank was immediately arrested. He was an old man who had spent most of his life in the National Archives gathering material for a scholarly study of colonial Spanish land grants. He had been appointed to the bank by Fuentes. He knew nothing about banking. He had merely carried out the orders of the Minister of Finance.

Fuentes had been his own Minister of Finance.

Interviewed on the subject by the press in Mexico City, ex-President Fuentes stated that the committee's revelations had shocked, horrified and amazed him. He also said that he had no idea where the missing twenty millions might be. Regrettably, he was unable quite to refrain from smiling as he said it.

Ex-President Fuentes' retirement has not been peaceful.

During the five years he held office as President there was only one serious attempt on his life. Since he resigned the Presidency, ceased to concern himself with politics and went to live abroad, no less than three such attempts have been made. There will doubtless be others. Meanwhile, he has had to fight off two lots of extradition proceedings and a number of civil actions directed against his European bank accounts.

He is wealthy, of course, and can afford to pay for the protection, both physical and legal, that he needs; but he is by no means resigned to the situation. As he is fond of pointing out, other men in his position have accumulated larger fortunes. Moreover, his regime was never unacceptably oppressive. He was no Trujillo, no Batista, no Porfirio Diaz. Why then should he be hounded and harrassed as if he were?

Ex-President Fuentes remains a puzzled and indignant man.

THE COMPANION

Joan Aiken

THE UGLINESS OF her rented cottage was a constant source of perverse satisfaction to Mrs Clyrard. To have travelled, in the course of her seventy-odd years, over most of the civilised world, to have lived in several of its most elegant capitals, and finally to have come to roost in Number Three, Vascoe's Cottages, had an incongruity that pleased her tart, ironic spirit. Mrs Clyrard indulged in a constant battle against life's unreasonablenesses and inequities. Her private hobby was finding fault—with the British government, the world's so-called leaders, with her bank, with her friends, with the young, the old, the stupid, the B.B.C. Third Programme, the weather, and the cakes from the village shop. It gave her intense, not wholly masochistic gratification to survey her hideous rented furniture, to go into her dark little unfunctional kitchen and discover that the gas-pilot had gone out again, that before putting a kettle on to boil she must laboriously poke a long-stemmed match into the dirty interstices of the stove, turn, at the same time, a small, gritty, and inconveniently-placed wheel, and wait for the resulting muffled explosion; this ritual, which often had to be enacted several times a day due to the fluctuations of gas pressure, filled her with a dour amusement, confirming, as it did, all her most pessimistic feelings about the world. The aged recalcitrant plastic ice-trays, which were most likely to split in half under pressure of an angry thumb than to eject a single cube of ice, the front gate that refused to latch properly, the wayward taps turning in improbable directions, emitting a thin thread of lukewarm water, the varying levels of the cottage, which had steps up or steps down between all its rooms, even one in the middle of the bathroom—these things fulfilled her expectation that life was intended to be a series of cynical boobytraps.

Nevertheless Mrs Clyrard could have lived in comfort if she had chosen. She was rich, had been married, had had a successful career as a painter, had had children even, now satisfactorily grown and disposed of; she was a handsome, intelligent, and cultivated woman; death had removed her husband, it was true, but otherwise she need have little to complain about; yet all possible amenities had been, it seemed, wantonly jettisoned in favour of retreat into the exile of a Cornish village. Not even romantic exile, for Talland was far from picturesque: it was a small, random conglomeration of ill-assorted, mostly granite, buildings established on a treeless hillside as if they had been dropped there.

Vascoe's Cottages, of which Mrs Clyrard occupied Number Three, had been a nineteenth-century addition; two pairs of plain red-brick semi-detached labourers' dwellings, which some hopeful later landlord's hand had embellished with heavy chalet-type ornamental woodwork, thereby further darkening the already inadequately-lit interiors.

"Oh, that will do for me very nicely," Mrs Clyrard had remarked with her usual brief smile, on first observing Number Three over its stout enclosing privet hedge.

"Are you certain?" her friend and prospective landlady Mrs Helena Soames doubtfully inquired. "Are you sure it will be big enough for you—*light* enough? The furniture is rather a job lot, I'm afraid. I could have it taken out, if you would like to put in your own things—"

"No, no, let them stay in store. I can't be bothered with them. This is admirable. And the furniture will last my time.

Mrs Clyrard was in excellent health, but she always spoke and acted as if in expectation of imminent death.

She moved herself into the cottage with a minimum of fuss or added impedimenta: a typewriter, some books; quickly learned the names and ways of the local tradespeople; and had soon established herself on terms of remarkable cordiality with all her neighbours; the terms being that she listened to—indeed, drew out by some unique osmosis of her own—all their dissatisfactions and complaints, meanwhile herself maintaining a considerable reticence. Complaint is addictive; people came back eagerly, again and again, for more; Mrs Clyrard had all the company she could have wished for. She listened, she made her own dry comments and never disbursed advice; this was the secret of her popularity. She never offered information about herself, or divulged her own feelings. If asked what she did with herself all day—for it was plain that she was neither house-proud nor a dedicated gardener—she replied.

"I am writing my memoirs. I have known any number of famous people—" and it was true, she had—"plenty of reputations will have the rug pulled from under them if I don't die before I have finished."

Although she frequently and drily referred to her possible death, she manifested no anxiety about the prospect, and seemed not particularly troubled as to whether she finished her memoirs first or not; very few things appeared to trouble Mrs Clyrard particularly; she found a sour pleasure in her occupations. Meanwhile the years rolled by, bestowing on her no signs of age or infirmity; nor did she manifest any disposition to seek more comfortable quarters than Number Three, Vascoe's.

"I don't know how you can endure the poky little place," Miss Morgan frequently remarked when she dropped in to complain about Mrs Soames. "It's so dark and cold. When I was living here with the old lady I thought I should go mad with the inconvenience. It must be the most awkward house in the world. Even with that lift installed."

The old lady had been Helena Soames's mother, Mrs Musgrave. For ten years prior to her death from heart disease she had occupied Number Three, Vascoe's, and Miss Morgan had been her companion. The lift had been installed for Mrs Musgrave's benefit; it consisted of a metal chair with a counterbalance, in the stairwell, operated by a small electric motor. Mrs Musgrave's son, an engineer, had installed it himself. The old lady had sat herself in the chair and been buckled in with a seat-belt; then she pressed a button and was conveyed slowly up or slowly down. The lift, with its ugly metalwork, still remained; but Mrs Clyrard, who had a rooted mistrust of all machinery, saw no occasion to make use of it.

After ten years Mrs Musgrave had died, and Miss Morgan, lacking a function, was removed to the manor to housekeep for the daughter, Mrs Soames—an arrangement which gave little satisfaction to either party.

Almost every day, at tea-time, Miss Morgan called in on Mrs Clyrard with some grievance to relate about Mrs Soames's fault-finding, heartlessness, inconsistency, or sarcasm, to which Mrs Clyrard listened with her usual acute impassivity.

"I do wish *you* would have me for your companion, dear Mrs Clyrard," Miss Morgan, who had a slight stammer, often sighed out. "I am s-sure we should get on so well! I would be so h-happy to look after everything for you while you wrote your memoirs, and would not dream of asking for a s-salary; all I want is a home."

"My dear woman, what possible use would I have for a companion in this tiny box of a house? I am almost too much company for myself."

Wispy, myopic little Miss Morgan would take herself off, pleading, "Think it over, dear Mrs Clyrard—do think it over!"

In the evenings Mrs Clyrard often heard the other side of the case: her friend Helena generally dropped in for a glass of sherry and a grumble about Miss Morgan's self-pity, inefficiency, forgetfulness, untidiness, tendency to martyrdom, and general inadequacy. Mrs Clyrard made no comment on that either. Nor did she see fit to intervene when Mrs Soames's patience finally ran out and she dismissed the unsatisfactory housekeeper, who, being far too old by now to secure another post, went lamenting away to live with her married sister in Lanlivery, after a final and unavailing plea to Mrs Clyrard to take her in.

More time went by. Mrs Clyrard lent a noncommittal ear to the outpourings of other neighbours: of harassed parents who could not deal with their young; of rebellious teenagers who could not endure their parents; of betrayed husbands; of frustrated wives; and of disillusioned friends who had fallen out. Her own private life remained as apparently tranquil as ever;

her excellently coiffed iron-grey hair turned a shade paler, her hawklike profile was unchanged; she wrote a few pages a day at the desk in her upstairs study, cooked light meals for herself, waged her usual guerrilla war against the inconveniences of her house, and continued in her customary state of sardonic composure.

But presently—and how it happened Mrs Clyrard was not precisely aware, for the change came by such gradual degrees—her equable daily routine became disrupted; not seriously, but just enough to be noticeable.

The form taken by the disturbance was this: Mrs Clyrard, seated upstairs in a state of recollected tranquillity at her typewriter, would suddenly find her concentration broken by an odd urge to go below and perform some slight unnecessary task in the kitchen. Sometimes her more rational self was able to withstand the trivial impulse; but sometimes it was not; and almost before she was aware of the process she would find herself at the kitchen sink washing teacloths; or cleaning the leaded glass panes in the front door (which made no difference to the light, for the untrimmed privet hedge grew within six feet of it); or polishing shoes, or defrosting the refrigerator.

This was very annoying, but Mrs Clyrard had no intention of submitting to it. She was a woman of total practicality. If she felt a twinge in a tooth, she consulted her dentist; if she detected a rattle in her car, she referred it to the garage. Possible psychic phenomena weighed no more and no less in her estimation than failures in the electrical system or mice in the pantry: as she would call in an electrician or a cat for the latter inconveniences, for the former she had recourse to an exorcist. Fortunately she was acquainted with one: an old friend of hers, a rural dean, living in semi-retirement in Bath, still took an active interest in para-normal occurrences, and occasionally officiated at a ceremony to remove some unwelcome or disturbed spirit.

Mrs Clyrard wrote and invited him for a visit, arranging to have him accommodated at a nearby guest-house, since she detested having people staying in the cottage.

When he arrived she lost no time explaining the nuisance to him.

"Somebody is trying to occupy my mind—or my house," she said matter-of-factly, though with a considerable degree of irritation. "I should be very much obliged if you could deal with it for me, Roger."

The dean, delighted with the odd problem, promised to see what he could do. To assist him, he fetched over a medium from Bath—a city much plagued by psychic phenomena, possibly due to its enclosed, low-lying, and damp situation.

The medium, Mrs Hannah Huxley, a portly, blind lady, acquiesced with the dean in taking the problem as a most serious challenge. They turned back the carpets, they inscribed formulae and diagrams repellent to invading spirits on the floors of all the rooms, they recited incantations, they lit candles and sprinkled water, they performed various rituals involving the doors, the windows, the curtains, the mirrors, the stairs, the fireplace, the lights. At one point during the proceedings, which were long, and to Mrs Clyrard somewhat tediously repetitious, Mrs Huxley went into a trance.

"Did your husband," she suddenly inquired, emerging from this condition as abruptly as she had gone into it, "did your husband die of a head injury, Mrs Clyrard?"

"Certainly not," said Mrs Clyrard with asperity, startled, and not best pleased at this intrusion into her private affairs. "He died of intestinal carcinoma."

"That's odd. I have distinct evidence of a presence quite close to you who has at some time suffered from a head injury. Are you quite sure that you can think of no such person?"

Mrs Clyrard moved a step or two aside, distastefully, before replying again.

"Absolutely not."

Her faith by now somewhat diminished, she watched in ironic silence as the dean and Mrs Huxley came to the conclusion of their ritual, having now apparently located the intrusive entity.

Kindly, cajoling, uttering mellifluous Latin phrases formed for the purposes of coaxing such undesired visitants from their lodgings, the dean walked slowly, backwards, beckoning, to the front door, opened it, waited, and recited a final prohibiting admonition before closing the door and returning to the fireside.

"There, it's gone!" he said with a beaming smile. "It can't come back inside now."

It? thought Mrs Clyrard, on an impulse of strong protest; how can that vague, unhappy, intrusive, indefinable emanation be compressed into and pinned down by such a brusque, particular little monosyllable as *it*?

"Poor thing, it simply hated to leave," the dean went on. "No, I'm afraid it didn't want to go in the very least. Did you hear it whimpering?"

Mrs Clyrard had not.

Stifling her scepticism, however, she civilly thanked the dean and his colleague, refreshed them after their exertions with tea and cakes from the village shop, conversed for a polite hour, and finally, with relief, saw them to the door and said goodbye. Still sceptical, but in a cool spirit of scientific investigation, she went upstairs for an experimental hour's writing. And the dean had been completely right, perfectly justified in his confidence: there was nothing to disturb her concentration; she found she could work in untroubled peace for the whole hour. Not a single thought of the tea-things waiting unwashed downstairs so much as slipped over the edge of her consciousness.

When Helena Soames presently arrived for a glass of sherry, at half past six, Mrs Clyrard was in a highly self-congratulatory state of mind and, contrary to her usual reticent habit, related the story.

"But I still can't imagine who the person suffering from a head injury can be," she concluded.

"Oh, can't you?" said Mrs Soames, who had listened with the greatest interest. "But it's perfectly obvious, my dear. It must be poor Miss Morgan."

"Miss *Morgan*? Did she have a head injury? I never knew of it."

"It was over before you came to the village, of course. In fact it happened while Miss Morgan was looking after my mother, in this cottage; after Edward had installed the chair-lift. Miss Morgan had strapped Mother in and then—stupid woman—stuck her head over the bannister to say, 'Is there anything you want me to bring you, Mrs Musgrave?' Of course the counterbalance came down, hit her on the head, and knocked her silly. She was never quite the same after that, but then she hadn't been too bright to start with. Luckily Mother died not long afterwards."

"Miss Morgan—yes, of course," said Mrs Clyrard reflectively, remembering the doleful little woman's plea to be allowed to return to the inconveniences of Number Three, Vascoe's. "I'd be so happy to look after the house for you while you wrote your memoirs. I wouldn't *dream* of asking for a salary. All I want is a home."

"It simply hated to leave," Roger had said. "It didn't want to go in the very least."

Looked at through those eyes the dark and poky sitting-room with its Tottenham Court Road furnishings momentarily took on the appearance of a warm and happy haven.

"Miss Morgan," Mrs Clyrard said again. "What became of her?"

"Oh, she went to live with that married sister in Lanlivery. The sister had always despised her. Miss Morgan didn't want to go, but what could she do? At her age she couldn't get another job. Anyway, evidently it was a disastrous arrangement, for about six months later I heard that she drowned herself in a brook. All for the best, really; as I said, she'd never been quite with it after that accident. Well, *you* must have noticed it—she used to come wailing round to you often enough."

"Yes. So she did," Mrs Clyrard said in the same thoughtful manner.

Miss Morgan: that melancholy, ineffectual little woman; ineffectual in death as in life, apparently.

Or was she?

Seeing Helena to the door, half an hour later, closing it briskly behind her, Mrs Clyrard was aware for the first time that the previous trivial though irritating mental distractions which had assailed her might have been exchanged for something even more unaccustomed: a sensation of discomposure, disquiet; perhaps even—to analyse it closely—fear?

For although the dean and Mrs Huxley had led the whimpering reluctant whatever-it-was along to the front door and out of the house, that was *all* they had done; they did not claim to have annihilated it, or driven it any farther than the threshold.

Mrs Clyrard allowed herself an uneasy glance at the door which framed its glass-paned square of dark.

Might not her visitor—out there in the little privet-enclosed garden—out there behind the glass-paned door in the rainy night—might it not feel, now, perhaps, a certain degree of *resentment* at its exclusion?

Mrs Clyrard heard the garden gate—which as usual had failed to latch properly—begin to creak and clatter as it swung to and fro in the rising wind.

She knew that she ought to go and fasten the gate before the hinges were damaged. And yet she lingered in the dreary little hallway, strangely reluctant to set foot outside the security of her house.

GIFTED AMATEURS

Kenneth Benton

NUMBER ELEVEN, ARCADIA Road, Fulham, was one of a uniform street of houses, solidly built but lacking charm, with a Victorian bay window, a tiled porch and stained glass panels in the front door. Across the street was its mirror image. The area had gone up in the world, and housed a proportion of professional people who had persuaded themselves that the formerly despised Victorian trimmings were really rather amusing. The interior white paint and plain coloured walls of Number Eleven stamped it as one of these.

Now, the double drawing-room had been cleared of armchairs, and the sofa and dining-table pushed back between the home-made bookcases that lined the walls. Mexican paper flowers were crammed into a pottery jar beside the fireplace and the three lamps whose shades reflected Cynthia Lockwood's past enthusiasms—one modern and textured, another made from a camel's stomach and the third a Tiffany of coloured glass—were lit. Cynthia herself was in the kitchen arranging the last canapés on peasant dishes.

Graham Jensen, a thickset man of twenty-six with a questing, intelligent face and fair hair brushed back to fall over the collar of his party suit, was pouring litre bottles of red, white and rosé wine into flagons and arranging glasses on the dining-table. He was the son of a primary school teacher in Nottingham, and had won a scholarship to Cambridge and later a Ph.D. for a thesis on cybernetics. James Lockwood was his boss and closest friend in London, and he was devoted to Cynthia. He was adjusting the level of a framed Art Nouveau poster when he heard steps in the hall and Cynthia came in, carrying a dish of canapés. Or rather, as usual, she made an entrance.

She paused, staring at Jensen with dark, expressive eyes. Beneath the straight fringe of her glossy page-boy cut, her level brows drew together in a frown. She was holding the dish in an outstretched hand, posing unconsciously in the wild silk caftan that fell sheer and gleaming from her shoulders.

Jensen gave her an amused, affectionate smile. "What've you got there, Salome? John the Baptist's head? Feeling guilty, are you?"

"I'm scared, Graham. I hope James hasn't done anything silly."

"He'll be all right. You'd better get that telephone call over, though."

In the dust-free, immaculate workshops of Consolidated Business Machines, off the motorway at Hounslow, the evening shift were working to the sound of piped pop music. They were women mostly, peering through heavy magnifiers at the connections, far finer than a human hair, they were welding to the minute transistors. In the administration tower the offices were empty except for the tenth floor, where lights shone out over the dark factory roofs. Sir John Holroyd, managing director of C.B.M. was working late. It was Monday, and a Dutch delegation would be arriving on Thursday to haggle over a contract—a very big one—for the purchase of the firm's latest and most sophisticated computer, and Sir John and Robin Landon, his sales director, were planning their campaign. The telephone rang, and Holroyd's P.A. spoke.

"It's Mrs Lockwood, Sir John."

He groaned. "Must I, Claire? I'm very busy."

"She sounds a bit worried. I think you'd better . . ."

"Oh all right, put her through." He was a tough businessman, self-made, and didn't like interruptions, least of all from the wife of his chief scientist. She overdramatised things intolerably—but then, she'd been on the stage before she married James, so perhaps she couldn't help it. All the same . . . "Yes, Cynthia, what can I do for you?"

"I'm sorry, Sir John, but have you still got James there?"

"No, I haven't. He was with us till about half past five, but then he left. Said he had to get back early because you had something on. Why?"

"He hasn't turned up. And he knows we've got guests arriving any moment now. I'm worried."

Holroyd glanced at his watch and threw up his eyes. "But it's only half past six, Cynthia. He's probably got into a traffic jam on the motorway or—" he shot a mischievous look at Landon—"or perhaps he's dropped in on that bird of his in the Cromwell Road, and she's kept him."

Very coldly she said, "That's not funny, Sir John."

"I'm sorry, my dear, it was just a silly joke. Of course I can see you're worried, but I'm sure it's just a jam, and he'll turn up." He put down the receiver. "That was stupid of me," he muttered ruefully. "She'll tell James, and I don't want him to have anything on his mind but how to explain the bloody Mark 14 circuits to the Dutch. It's their Professor Huykens who's going to swing the deal. If he can't be persuaded that the machine is as new and revolutionary as we say it is, you won't get the contract, Robin."

"I can explain it, sir."

"No, you can't, my lad. Your job is prices and conditions. You can't talk binary mathematics, but James can. Let's get back to work."

They were still working, and Holroyd had sent his P.A. home, when the telephone rang again. Wearily, Sir John picked up the receiver. He could hear a chinking of glasses and the sound of chatter in the background. Cynthia's voice was low, but with clear signs of panic. He stifled a curse. "What is it now?" he asked curtly.

"A man rang, just a few minutes ago. He said James was safe, but wouldn't be coming home tonight. He asked me how he could get hold of you, and I gave him this number."

"Oh, for God's sake . . ."

"Listen, Sir John, it's serious. He sounded Irish, and said—he said it was a *snatch*."

Holroyd sat upright. "Go on, Cynthia," he said quietly. "Tell me exactly what he said." He signed to Landon to pick up the duplicate receiver.

"He said—well, he said you'd pay up. But if you got in touch with the cops he'd know, and James would be in trouble—and so would your contract. I don't know what he meant, but that was it, exactly." Cynthia's voice was hysterical. "I'm so scared for him, Sir John. For heaven's sake do what the man wants and don't tell the police. I haven't—in fact I've said nothing to anyone except Graham. He's here with me."

He replied slowly and reassuringly. "You've done quite right. Tell Graham Jensen to keep his mouth shut. Now don't worry, Cynthia. I'll wait and see what this fellow wants. I'll ring you later."

He hung up and spoke to Landon. "You heard that. James has been hi-jacked and they're going to twist my balls until I pay up. They must know our situation pretty well, and it may be an inside job, so get hold of Personnel and start thinking who it could be. Anyone who is in the know and has a grudge. Start with James's assistants in Research. Stop." He waved Landon back to his seat. "I haven't finished. Ring someone in Scotland Yard on another line and throw your weight about. Security should be able to tell you who to get hold of. Emphasise the importance of this contract for U.K. export figures. Get them to send a responsible bloke to my house at nine tonight precisely. Plain clothes, of course. I'll see the street door's open and he can come straight in. One more thing. Get me a new cassette from next door, so I can tape all conversations on this phone. That's it. Scarper!"

Holroyd had iron nerves, and after Landon had gone he returned to his papers. It was twenty minutes before the telephone rang, and he switched on the tape-recorder, which was connected with the receiver.

The voice was high-pitched but muffled, with an Irish brogue. "Is that Sir John Holroyd?" "It is." "Then listen, boyo." There was a slight whirr, then James Lockwood's voice, strained, artificial, but unmistakable.

"This is Lockwood, Sir John. The men who're holding me know about the Dutch deal. They will release me tomorrow night if by then you have paid them twenty thousand pounds value in industrial diamonds. You will get a call tomorrow morning, at the office, at ten o'clock. You must not inform the police. They say they—they will kill me if you do and just disappear. I am sure they mean business. You must tell them you agree when they call you, and do what they say, exactly. Tell Cynthia I'm all right, please. Make sure you do that." There was a click, and the muffled voice spoke again. "Did you get that Holroyd, or do I have to play it through to you again?"

"I got it. But look here..." The telephone went dead.

Cliveden Place is that part of the King's Road which connects Sloane Square and Eaton Square. On its south side are large Georgian houses, lying back from the busy thoroughfare. Sir John Holroyd's home was one of these, with the drawing-room facing the road, and it was from this room that, at nine o'clock exactly, he saw a man walk up to the gate. He slipped out into the hall and unlatched the front door, standing back as the man came in.

He was in his thirties, dressed in a well-cut suède jacket and whipcord trousers, a self-confident young man, bland and cheerful. If he sometimes gave an impression of guileless bonhomie, it was misleading. It misled Holroyd, and his face fell. "I understood the Yard was sending a senior officer," he said shortly.

"Detective Inspector Randolf, sir. Fraud Squad. I've had a lot of experience of snatch cases. But if you want to ring my boss, it's Commander Robbins, and I'll give you his home number."

"There's no time," said Sir John irritably. "You'll have to do. The kidnapper rang again and I've got a record of what passed between us. But let me make this clear," he added, as he showed Randolf into the library at the back of the house, "this is an awkward case. Sit down. Before I play back the tape let me explain. Doctor Lockwood..."

The Inspector raised his hand. "Excuse me. I know Doctor Lockwood is invaluable to you, especially at this time. Mr Landon made that clear. He also said you had assured Mrs Lockwood you wouldn't inform the police."

"That's not correct. I made no promise either way."

"Well, sir, I'm very glad you did decide to call us in. Just one question. Was I right in saying Lockwood is invaluable, I mean literally irreplaceable at this juncture?"

"The short answer is yes. I can explain in detail if you wish." He was placing the tape-recorder on the table as he spoke.

"Thank you, sir. Let's hear the record." He listened as Holroyd ran through the taped conversation, then said, "If the kidnappers are skilled and careful there's always the risk, however slight, that they may spot that we're on the job, and the further risk that they may—I won't say kill Lockwood, but hold him for several days while they try to shake us off. Would such a delay affect your position?"

"It would indeed. The Dutch team are going to the States if they can't conclude a deal here, and we have keen American competition. Delay must be avoided at all costs. I must have Lockwood back at latest by tomorrow night, and if necessary I'm perfectly prepared to pay the sum demanded. I've already been in touch with members of my board and have their agreement."

Randolf raised his eyebrows. "You know, sir," he said with a slight smile, "I'm a little surprised that you did bring us in."

Holroyd exploded. "What the hell d'you mean? This kind of thing couldn't happen if you people had your wits about you. Of course I want you to catch them and send them down for a long stretch." He stopped suddenly, and smiled. "I'm sorry. In fact, I could say I was public-spirited in taking the risk—and I realise how big the risk is—but it isn't citizenship or anything like that. I just want to get my own back on the buggers for the trouble they're giving me."

"We'll do our best, sir. Can you get hold of the diamonds?"

"No problem. We use industrials in the factory. And that's another thing the bastards know. I can get a parcel made up first thing tomorrow morning by our Hatton Garden suppliers."

"I see, sir. But I suggest you don't agree to any hand-over until after dark tomorrow. Try to make it after six. That'll give me time to arrange the surveillance under cover of at least partial darkness." The Chief Inspector got to his feet. "He said he would call you tomorrow morning at ten, at Hounslow. Would you please ring me as quickly as possible afterwards, at this extension, on the Yard Number 230 1212, and use your direct line, if you have one. Not through your exchange."

Holroyd nodded, and let the Chief Inspector out into the street.

At ten minutes past ten o'clock the following morning Holroyd rang Randolf at the Yard. "I'm speaking on my direct line, and there's no one about."

"Good. What did he say, sir?"

"It was the same voice you heard last night. I agreed to his demand and said I'd have the parcel of diamonds ready this evening by six o'clock. He said to be in my house, with the package, and I'd get instructions between six and half past, by telephone. He didn't ask for the number, which—" Holroyd's voice rang harshly—"is ex-directory. It *is* one of my own people who's tipped them off. I'd like to lay my hands on him."

"Anything else, sir?"

"Yes. I was to have the car ready to leave, with a full tank. I suppose they want to be sure I'm not followed."

"Could be," said Randolf thoughtfully. "But if it's only that, they're amateurs."

"Why?"

"Because if they think you may have contacted us after all they ought to know we'd supply you with a radio contact, so that you could let the Q cars know where you were heading. You still haven't told anyone else, apart from Mr Landon, that we're in the picture?"

"No. In fact, I've been getting cold feet about having contacted you at all. Unless you can assure me that there won't be the smallest risk that the kidnappers spot your presence, we'd better drop the whole idea."

"Let's discuss my plans this evening. If I come to your house well before the expected call, say about four o'clock, will your wife or someone be there to let me in?"

"She's abroad, but the housekeeper will be warned. I'll say you're a friend, and that I hope not to keep you waiting long.

O.K.?" He paused. "I'll try to get there by about twenty to six."

"That's fine, sir. Have you picked on anyone in your office whom we ought to have a look at?"

"No. There's only one person, but he's in the clear. I'll explain later, when we meet."

When Sir John let himself into his house that evening Randolf was sitting comfortably in an armchair in the library, with the remains of a substantial tea beside him, reading *The Times*. He got to his feet.

"Sit down." Holroyd sank into a chair and produced from his pocket a small package. "Doesn't look very big, does it? But there's twenty thousand pounds worth. It wasn't quite as easy as I expected."

Randolf glanced at his watch. "We've got some time to spare. Who was it, sir, who you said might have been suspect?"

"Graham Jensen, Lockwood's assistant. He's a first-class scientist, and very bright. Almost as smart as Lockwood. They did a tour of the Dutch factories a few months ago and Jensen wrote the report. Very impressive, too. But he's a bit bolshie. Agin' the Establishment, that sort of thing, and inclined to shoot his mouth off about it." He saw the trace of a superior smile on Randolf's face. "Don't get me wrong. I know that's not unusual these days, but I couldn't help thinking. . . . Jensen is very ambitious, and knows the mathematics of the Mark 14 almost as well as Lockwood. In theory he mightn't be too unhappy if James was out of the way and he had to step into the breach."

Randolf nodded. "It's a motive, isn't it?"

"But it doesn't fit, and I'll tell you why. When Cynthia rang me last night and told me about the call she'd just had from the Irishman, or whoever it was, Jensen was there with her."

"That doesn't prove he isn't involved," objected Randolf. "There could be the Irishman as well."

"That's true. But my main reason is simply that I can't imagine Jensen playing such a dirty trick on Lockwood. He admires him and his wife enormously, and their house is almost a second home for him."

"H'm. Could you tell me something about the Lockwoods, sir?"

Holroyd sighed. "I was speaking to Cynthia just now. I don't usually have much time for the girl, but she's made me feel really sorry for her. She's obviously under great strain. That's one reason. . . . You see, if it should turn out I did the wrong thing, calling in the police she'd never forgive me. And that means Lockwood, too, if he comes out of this alive. He's under her thumb, of course."

"Of course, sir?"

"Good heavens, man, he's just a scientist. He doesn't know which socks he's wearing. She looks after him like a child."

"And yet you'd wish him to play a vital part in your negotiations with the Dutch. Surely, from what you've said, Jensen would do the job just as well?"

"It's quite simple. I wouldn't let Jensen touch it. He's very clever and knows his stuff, but he's brash, undiplomatic and above all very young, and looks it. He'd get short shrift from Professor Huykens, the Dutch scientist. Whereas once you get James talking about his own brainchild—it was he who designed the Mark 14—he's lucid, persuasive, tactful—everything a negotiator ought to be. That's what makes him so invaluable."

"And I suppose you pay him a very handsome salary?"

Holroyd glanced at the police officer suspiciously. "What are you getting at?"

"I live in Fulham, too, and I had a quick look at their house this morning. Just routine. It doesn't strike me as the home of affluent people, but perhaps I'm wrong."

"My dear fellow," said Holroyd irritably, "scientists are scientists. They have the ideas, some good, some bad, and we buy their services, but it's the engineers and businessmen who make and sell the product, and they're proportionately better paid. But don't get the impression James isn't pretty well off. The trouble is that he doesn't seem able to save. If they do sell their house, as they want to, they'll get a good price for it, but they'll never be able to buy the sort of place Cynthia wants. She was on the stage, you know, and she's got grand ideas. Her sights are always set too high. Luckily," added Holroyd, with a complacent smile, "James Lockwood doesn't give a hoot, as long as he's within reach of his precious labs. Now then, what are we going to do when this bastard rings?"

"I've already got a surface tap on your receiver, so I'll be listening in." He opened a briefcase that lay on the floor by his chair and brought out a hand-sized transceiver. "Keep this in your coat pocket, but don't try to use it where you might be seen. In your car it'll be O.K. I'll be behind you in my blue Cortina, but you won't see me. Just keep in touch and tell me where you're going. Don't forget to pull out the antenna, though. Like this."

"Is it just you, or are there other men with you?"

"There's another car, and a man on foot, at present skulking round the corner in Bourne Street until I give him the word by radio. That is just in case you have to go on foot."

The telephone bell rang, and as Holroyd picked up the receiver Randolf screwed a plastic plug into his ear. The voice said, "Have you got the parcel?"

"I have it here."

"Then keep it with you, mister," said the muffled voice. "You're not going in any bleeding car, but on your flat feet. Leave now, *at once*. Walk into Sloane Square. Inside the station you'll see the second telephone box has an OUT OF ORDER sign on it. Forget that and go inside. At the back of the A–D directory you'll find where you have to go. But leave now, as I said, or there'll be throubble.'

"I'll leave at once."

The phone went dead. When Holroyd turned round Randolf was already speaking into his radio. He finished, and said tersely, "Blast them! They've made it awkward. But you'll be followed. When you get into the call-box, if it's dark enough for you to do it unobserved, take out your radio and tell me what the instructions are. If it isn't possible, go where the man says, but not too fast."

"And you're sure . . .?"

"We'll be very, very careful."

It was only a short walk for Holroyd to make in the rain, but he hated every minute of it. He had a small fortune in jewels in his pocket—but what if the kidnappers hung on to Lockwood and asked for more? They had him over a barrel. . . .

At the corner of Sloane Square he hesitated for a moment, looking across at the dripping plane trees and the empty taxi rank. The last of the rush-hour crowd were scurrying into the station. Holroyd passed the pub and the Royal Court Theatre and peered into the lighted booking-hall. Several people were waiting outside one of the call-boxes, but the next one, true enough, bore the OUT OF ORDER notice. He pushed his way through the hurrying commuters and entered the box. There was light enough without turning the switch and he pulled up the A–D directory on its hinge and opened the back cover. Inside, on a sheet of toilet paper, words had been scrawled with a felt pen: *Leave the package behind the books and hop it. Don't turn round, or else—!!!*

Holroyd thrust the paper into his pocket with his gloved hand, and felt the little radio. But there was too much light. Anyone standing near him could see him use it. Cursing, he left the set where it was and pulled out the parcel of diamonds, wedged it behind the directories, and left the box. He did as he had been told, and walked straight out into the street. Two minutes later he was at home. He took out the radio, extended the antenna and switched the set on. "Randolf, are you there?"

"Yes, sir. What happened?"

Holroyd told him. There was a blasphemous muttering at the other end, then Randolf said, "They've outsmarted us, sir. But I'll see what my chap has to say. I'll be along."

He rang the bell shortly afterwards and Holroyd let him in. "Well?"

Randolf sighed. "The man I had trailing you was standing just inside the entrance, as ordered, so that when you came out of the call-box he could follow you either into the square or down the stairs to the trains, whichever you'd been instructed to do. He saw you leave the station and followed you, unfortunately. But as he waited for you to pass him he did see something else. A man went into the OUT OF ORDER box and came out again quickly. Then he ran through the barrier towards the stairs that go down to the westbound platform. Medium height, shaggy fair hair and beard, wearing jeans and a long sheepskin coat with a white C.N.D. sign daubed on the back. That's all my man saw, and he didn't attach any significance to it. It looked like someone who'd ignored the notice and tried the phone on spec. I've sent him back, of course, but it'll be too late, though he might just find someone who could say which train the man with the coat had taken. I'm sorry, sir; I should have thought of this gimmick, but it's damned awkward, having to be so careful."

Holroyd said gruffly, "You did your best." The telephone rang and he picked up the receiver. "It's for you."

Randolf listened for a moment or two, his mouth hardening. He said, "O.K. Report to me here," and hung up. He turned to Holroyd.

"He found the coat," he said shortly.

"Well, that's something. Where was it?"

"The D.C. couldn't see anyone like the subject on the platform, so before asking questions he tried the little bar. There was the coat, lying over a chair in the corner. No one had seen who'd left it there." He sighed. "That's wrecked our last chance of picking him up at any of the Underground stations. I had a call put out before I came in. The chap probably had a plastic mac in his pocket. Jeans and face fungus are far too common, nowadays. People might notice a distinctive coat, but hardly a plastic mac."

"But the coat?"

"I expect he bought it at an Oxfam shop for next to nothing and used it this once. It's no good, sir; I've boobed. Let's only hope they keep their end of the bargain."

Sir John gave a wry smile. "As long as they send Lockwood back I don't care. I'll get you a drink."

Later, when Randolf and his wife were just settling down to watch the ten o'clock news on I.T.V., Sir John telephoned to say that Lockwood was at home and well. "I'm going to the Lockwoods' place now, and I'll pick you up if you give me your address."

Waiting in the street for Holroyd's Daimler to arrive Randolf was forming a clear picture of how the interview should go. He would handle the Lockwoods with tact and finesse and draw out all those significant bits of detail that would put him on the trail of the snatchman. The car drew up, and the sight of two bottles of champagne on the back seat made Randolf uneasy; this was no time for celebration.

When Sir John introduced him Cynthia Lockwood stiffened, but Holroyd produced the champagne and pushed past her to greet her husband like a prodigal son. Jensen stood up, smiling.

As they gathered, chatting happily, round Sir John, who was opening the wine, Randolf wandered around the room. It was the first time he had seen the Lockwoods and he was trying unobtrusively to size them up. Cynthia, animated, enjoying the sympathy of the three men for her long ordeal. Tough, though, he'd say. Lockwood, tall and gangling, with a thin nervous face. A two-day beard added to the impression of strain, but made one wonder why he hadn't had time to shave after his adventure. He was dressed in a drooping fisherman's sweater and shabby slacks. Brainy, thought Randolf, as you'd expect, but no fighter. Jensen was obviously completely at home with the Lockwoods. That young man would always be keen to show he was on the ball. The first kid to put his hand up at school. Memories of a hated class-mate flashed through Randolf's mind.

Lockwood, amiable but cautious, moved towards Randolf with a glass of champagne in his hand, which he offered.

"No, thank you, sir. I'm still on duty."

"Of course. I—er—didn't expect to have to deal with the police, after that message for Sir John the kidnappers made me record. But he says he felt he had to call you in."

"Not," put in Cynthia disdainfully, "that it made the slightest difference."

"That's not necessary, Cynthia," said Holroyd sharply. "I had no choice. The board would have thought it very remiss of me if I hadn't done so. You must see that Inspector Randolf still has a job to do."

"I have indeed, madam." He turned to Lockwood. "You said kidnappers, sir. There was more than one, then?"

"There were two. Fergus and the one with the coat. I didn't catch his name." He sat down beside his wife on the sofa, with a weary sigh.

Randolf took a chair opposite them and brought out his notebook. "Now that's interesting, sir. Fergus, eh? Were they both Irish, then?"

"Oh yes, it was obvious."

"Well, that's something. I'd got the impression that the accent on the telephone was faked. Now, sir, would you mind telling me exactly what happened to you?"

"Of course." The other two men were seated now, and listening. Lockwood took a sip of champagne and began the story, speaking rapidly and without hesitation. He had left the office in the administration block at half past five and had collected his Ford Escort from the garage. He gave its description and number, adding that it still hadn't turned up, as he would explain later. He had driven out of the factory precinct towards the motorway and almost at once saw what he thought at first was one of the company's men, waiting for a lift. He often gave such persons a ride into the West End, and stopped to pick him up. "He looked a bit hairy, literally, with a ragged beard and a sort of shepherd's coat that came down half way to his ankles, but one gets used to this sort of dress. Long dark hair, and a cloth cap. He didn't say much, but once we were out on the motorway, just before the Chiswick flyover, he pulled out a gun and told me to turn off or he'd shoot. Frankly, I was scared. It was the real thing, I'm sure of that." Lockwood yawned. "Excuse me, but I feel so tired. I suppose it's the reaction. You go on, darling; I've told it all to you already."

Before she could speak Randolf raised his hand. "If you don't mind, sir, I'd rather hear you tell the story. There might be significant little bits that come into your mind as you talk. Go on, please. Can't you add to that description? After all, anyone could wear a false beard and a hairy coat, couldn't they?"

Lockwood looked annoyed. "But Sir John's just told us you'd got someone who saw the man as he ran away."

"He only got a fleeting glimpse, sir, and if we're to catch our villains we want descriptions as good as we can get."

"Oh, I see. Well, what else? Oh yes, he was about middle height, not tall. Grey eyes, bony face—what you could see of it for all the hair. He wore gloves . . ."

"All the time he was with you?"

"While he was in my car, anyway. And when he took off the coat in the caravan he was wearing jeans and a zip-up leather jacket. O.K., then," he continued irritably, as he saw Randolf about to speak. "Blue jeans, patched and much worn, and the jacket was black. I forgot. There was a C.N.D. sign in white on the back of his coat, the long one he wore in the car. And the cap was the kind Chancellor Schmidt wears. Northern European, if you know what I mean."

"You're doing fine, sir. What happened when you turned off?"

"I stopped, and he made me get out, come round the car and get into the passenger seat. He had the gun pointing the whole time, but with his other hand he brought out a pair of handcuffs and made me put one on and click it shut, then lay my other wrist in the cuff while he locked it." He paused. "But first I'd had to pass the chain through the seat support rail. So you see I was bent double, with my hands near the floor. So I couldn't see. Then he took the driver's seat."

"No one about?"

"No, and it was dark."

"You must show me on the map," said Randolf, "but wait a moment." He bent down as he sat in his chair, lowered his hands to within six inches of the floor and raising his head peered forward. "You'd still see through the windscreen."

"I couldn't, you know," said Lockwood obstinately. "I saw damn' all. I couldn't see where he took me."

"After all, James," put in Jensen, "you told us earlier he took your glasses."

"That was it, of course. You see, without my specs I'm

almost blind. I'm sorry, Inspector, but I really am tired and I get a bit confused."

"I shan't be long, sir. I hope. Which way did you go? East or West?"

"Westwards, about ten miles I should think, about a quarter of an hour. Then he turned off to the left and it began to get increasingly dark as the street lights thinned out, and then quite empty of lights and we stopped while he opened a gate, and then we bumped across a field and landed up alongside the caravan. A second man came up to the car, and he had a gun, too. Description? Oh, taller than the first one, wearing a blue anorak and slacks, with a stocking over his head. This fellow unlocked the handcuffs . . ."

"Had he a key of his own?"

"What? No, the first one passed him the key through the car window. The second man, Fergus, pushed me into the van and made me lie down on one of the bunks, and this time he put the handcuffs round my ankles and attached them to the bottom of the bunk."

"To the frame, I suppose?"

"Yes, of course. There was a curved bar at the end of the bed."

"Curious," said Randolf, making a note with a large question mark against it. "I mean, I don't remember seeing bunks like that—almost like iron beds—in a caravan."

"Can't all this wait till the morning?" interjected Sir John suddenly. "It's after eleven, and we've all got to get some sleep."

"I'll be as quick as I can, sir. Let's leave the interior of the van for the time being. What happened to the first man?"

"He was already driving off in my car while I was being pushed up the steps into the van. I suppose he must have changed the number plates, just in case the police had been tipped off."

"They couldn't have been, darling," said Cynthia. "You must have got to the caravan about . . ."

"Between seven and half past, I should think."

"That's what I mean. It was only at half past seven that the man rang me and told about kidnapping you."

"Oh, yes. Well, he came back about an hour later, while Fergus was cooking in the galley. We had supper, sausages and mash. And tinned beer. After that they let me go to the loo, one of those chemical ones, and then locked me up again. They'd given me back my glasses and a few thrillers to read, and while I slept they took turns, one on the opposite bunk, the other on guard, with the gun. The blinds were drawn, of course. There were no lights visible outside." Lockwood picked up his champagne glass, which had been re-filled twice, and drained it, passing a hand over his eyes.

Randolf smiled. "I'm tired, too, sir. I'd love a cup of tea, if Mrs Lockwood would be so kind."

She stood up slowly, looking down at her husband. "I suppose so," she said coldly, and went out into the kitchen.

Randolf said suddenly, "Were you warm enough?"

"Warm? Oh yes. Although the van wasn't heated they had blankets. I was quite comfortable."

"Except for your feet, surely?"

"What d'you mean?"

"Only that if they were handcuffed to the bar at the end of the bed they must have been pressed up against cold metal all night."

There was a pause. Both Jensen and Holroyd were about to speak when Lockwood said, "I'll show you something." He bent forward, pulled up his slacks and rolled his socks down, pointing to two broad yellow rings round his ankles. "Cynthia paints everything with iodine," he explained with a faint grin. "It hurt like hell."

"I see, sir. Well, there's a lot more detail I shall want from you tomorrow, but let's call it a day, shall we? Or just the last bit. What happened today?" He smiled encouragingly. "Just the significant bits."

"The first man was out all day, and I was alone with Fergus. We played chess, but he wasn't very good and lost his temper. The other man came back about seven, very pleased with himself, and showed us the parcel of diamonds, and we all had beer. Then he said he would keep his part of the bargain, and unlocked me from the bed. It was dark outside, but there was a red Mini there, and he made me sit in the front passenger seat and locked my wrists as before to the support rail under the seat, and took my glasses away. He said he'd go back and drive my own car to an overnight car park, and post me the ticket. I suppose I'll get it tomorrow. He drove me to Ruislip station underground. They hadn't touched my money, luckily."

There were sounds from the direction of the kitchen. Quickly, Randolf pretended to consult some earlier notes in his book. "Was the man who drove you to Ruislip still wearing the same clothes? Hadn't he changed the leather jacket for a red sweater?"

"He may have done," said Lockwood wearily. "I told you, he wore this woolly coat when he was out of doors. I couldn't see."

There was a sharp rattle of crockery. Cynthia was bringing in a cup of tea. "I'm so sorry," she said. "I've slopped it into the saucer." Then she turned to Lockwood. "I thought you told us, James," she said quietly, with a steely undertone, "that the man hadn't got his shepherd's coat when he came back to the caravan this evening."

He started. "Of course, that's right," he said quickly. "How stupid of me. Nor he had."

"Then what," asked Randolf patiently, "was he wearing above the waist?"

Lockwood hesitated. Cynthia said, "The leather jacket. That's what James told us earlier."

"I see." Randolf turned to Lockwood. "You of course don't know, but in fact, the coat was dumped in Sloane Square station after the hand-over of the ransom. It's an old trick to deceive the surveillance. You wear something very distinctive, so that the trailer will fix on that, and then you just shed it somewhere. I've got the coat in my keeping, for the moment, but I didn't bring it here. It smells to high heaven." He turned his cold eyes on Cynthia Lockwood. "And I don't mean sheepskin, madam. I mean body odour. And quite disgusting."

Cynthia gave a gasp of outrage. "But that's imposs . . ." she began, but stopped with her hand over her mouth. A deep flush spread over her pale face.

Jensen was on his feet, and furious. "That's a dirty fuzz trick if I ever saw one. It was . . ."

To Randolf's extreme annoyance, Holroyd stopped further indiscretions. "Be quiet," he shouted, "and let the Inspector finish his task and go."

Randolf was still watching Cynthia Lockwood. "How could you know it was impossible, Mrs Lockwood? Unless you bought the coat—*and wore it?*"

She burst into tears, turned to her husband and threw herself into his arms. He stroked her dark hair gently, then faced Randolf. "Whatever fanciful ideas you may have in your nasty little mind, Inspector, you can tell them to me, not my wife."

Randolf was put out. The man was transformed. He was now fighting for survival, and for his wife, and he would fight hard. But the Inspector was determined not to have his prize snatched away from him. "It seems clear to me, sir, that you and Mrs Lockwood have been deceiving me—and your employer. It would be easier if you admitted it now. You won't like the alternative."

"Nonsense! You haven't the slightest evidence to support that slanderous suggestion. If you have, tell me."

"No evidence, sir, as yet, just indications." His voice rose menacingly. "But when we've compared those long dark hairs on the collar of the sheepskin coat with your wife's; when we've taken this house apart and collected everything worth examining microscopically—the clothes you were wearing yesterday, for example, and the contents of the U traps in the plumbing and the household waste-bins . . ." Lockwood's face was wooden, but Randolf heard a moan from Cynthia. He smiled. "You see, another indication. She didn't think of that when she cleaned off that nasty beard. Then there's your car, if it turns up. That would tell us a lot. And incidentally, I must point out that the front seats of a Mini don't run on rails, but are hinged. Then there's the voice-print we'll make of that faked Irish voice . . ."

"He's bluffing," shouted Jensen. "They can't *do* that, Cynthia."

"There's a lot we can do that you may not know about, Doctor Jensen." Randolf turned to Lockwood. "We shall find the evidence, I assure you. Your best course is to make a true statement now. Mrs Lockwood, be sensible. It's in your own interest to tell the truth."

She sat up, wearily, and reached into her bag for a handkerchief. "It's no good, James . . ."

But Sir John Holroyd was speaking, with quiet authority. "Until I've finished what I want to say, I want no interruptions, please." Randolf was uneasy. He had an idea of what was going to happen, and he had to try to stop it. He stood up. "I have strong grounds for suspicion, Sir John, but I must arrange at once for a warrant to search these premises." He was pulling his radio set from his breast pocket as he spoke.

"Sit down, please. And you, too, James. Let me have my say, Inspector, and you can then do what you want. I have no wish to obstruct the due process of law. That's better. Now listen, all of you. Inspector Randolf has done us a service," he continued blandly. "He's shown us where we stand. He evidently thinks it likely that the whole of this kidnap plot was hatched by Doctor and Mrs Lockwood, and that she played the part of the person who took the ransom. But I wouldn't want him to get his fingers burnt. You see, Inspector, even if you could find hard evidence of what you suspect, surely it was a harmless prank." Sir John ignored the expressions of complete bewilderment on the faces of his audience. "In any case, that is the attitude I should take, and I assure you that in no circumstances would I press charges. Provided, of course, that the diamonds are returned to the company, and promptly. I am sure we should allow those who carried out this unfortunate hoax to come to their senses and return the stones. Once that is done, I am convinced we can all let the matter die a natural death."

"The police could bring charges," said Randolf harshly, "and you, Sir John, could be subpoenaed as a prosecution witness."

Holroyd looked at his watch. "It is well after midnight. I doubt if you'd get a search warrant at this time of night, particularly if I ring the duty officer in your Squad at the Yard and make it clear that in my opinion you are exceeding your duty, and that if you persist it will imperil a transaction of great importance to the national export drive."

There was complete silence in the room. Then Holroyd turned to Lockwood, "You see, James, I do very much value your vital *and continuing* role in the company. I really can't afford to do without you. I may have been thoughtless in the past. There was that matter of the loan you wanted for buying a new house!"

"You could have granted it, couldn't you?" growled Lockwood.

"It was difficult, because of the Board, but there's no doubt I could persuade them now. Twenty thousand pounds at nominal interest, wasn't it?"

"Twenty thousand pounds," repeated Randolf, with a sneer. "There's a coincidence for you!"

Sir John ignored him. "Yes, James, you won't have to worry about that. I can see now that a problem like that can drive a man to do very strange things. I want you fully concentrated on your job."

Lockwood smiled. "Yes, sir." Cynthia glowered.

"Then I'll be on my way. But I'd better get that call to the Yard over first, unless . . ." He looked at Randolf.

The Inspector got up slowly. "I'd like a word with you, sir. But it can wait until we're in the car."

As they went out into the street they heard bolts slide into place and the rattle of a chain. Sir John took the Inspector's reluctant arm. "They'll be unscrewing the U traps and ransacking the waste," he said, laughing. "Just between ourselves, Randolf, you slipped up, didn't you?"

"Did I not?" replied the Inspector, as he got into Sir John's car. "I ought to have just listened, and left them thinking they were in the clear. Above all, I shouldn't have let you know what I suspected. Then I'd have been round there tomorrow with a search warrant, without your knowing a thing about it. It'd have been a pleasure." He groaned. "What a bloody mess I've made of it!"

"I can perhaps help you there. I shall ring the Assistant

Commissioner tomorrow, say I'm convinced the whole thing was planned as a silly prank, and that the stones are being returned. As they will be, I haven't the smallest doubt. I shall make the point about the importance of this contract, of course, and explain how awkward it would be if the police pressed charges, and also that if that happened I would provide top-grade legal assistance to the Lockwoods. But I shall also say some very nice things about you. And I mean that. If you ever wanted to leave the Force for a civilian security job . . ."

"I'm not open to bribery, sir, and I shan't fudge my report."

"You've got me all wrong. I admit you made a bloomer earlier in the evening, but the way you tackled them roused my genuine admiration." He chuckled. "And very unscrupulous, some of it. That crack about B.O., for instance."

"There was a faint whiff of expensive perfume, sir. Nothing more."

"Masterly! Where d'you suppose the diamonds are? In the house?"

"No, I don't think they'd be as stupid as that. Although I suspect Jensen was in on the planning of the whole thing I don't think he played an active part. But he could have taken charge of the stones. That woman did the real job. I don't suppose Lockwood did more than drive into the country somewhere, and put up at a pub. I imagine," he added with a cynical laugh, "that you're going to use him to land this contract, and then sack him?"

"Good heavens, no. If he can convince the Dutch experts, as I'm sure he will, I'll give him a rise in salary. The bastard! In business, Randolf, we're used to nurturing vipers in our bosom. But some day," added Sir John grimly, "I'll get my own back on that precious pair, don't you worry. Tell me, what put you on to them first?"

Randolf expanded. "In my job, sir, you get a sort of nose for deceit. It was the stage Irish on the telephone, partly; the real micks don't talk that way, so I guessed the accent was assumed. So when Lockwood testified that they really *were* Irish, my nose began to twitch. Then the slight scent on the coat had indicated that the wearer might have been a woman, although you can never tell these days. Then Lockwood gave his evidence, if you can call it that, exactly as if he'd learned it by heart. But he really was under strain, so when he forgot a bit his wife had to prompt him. And there were such gaps. Did you notice he never even mentioned when and how he recorded that message which was played over to you? He said the chap who'd snatched him went off as soon as he'd delivered his captive to the caravan. No time for any recording. And the whole of the description of the van and the car drives sounded phoney. A man in that position makes at least some guess where he's being taken. Lockwood didn't even count the traffic signals. Then there was the mistake about the Mini. They are two-door, and the seats hinge. Oh, and a lot of little things. My suspicions became so strong that forgetting you might have no interest in seeing justice done I laid a trap and they all fell into it. Bloody fool! I ought to have known better." He thought for a moment. "They had the ideas, all right, but no experience of crime, so they fluffed the execution of their plan. Just amateurs!"

"*Gifted* amateurs," murmured Sir John, as if to himself.

"Only thanks to you, sir."

Randolf was not amused.

THE DECLINE AND FALL OF MR BEHRENS

Michael Gilbert

WHEN MR BEHRENS had got into it, it had been an Underground train, and full of people. Now, emerging into the pale sunlight of a late January afternoon, shedding passengers at every stop, it was pottering unhurried and almost empty through the flat countryside of the Thames delta; past stations whose names ended romantically in Tree and Wood and Park, but which exhibited an unbroken vista of bricks and mortar; past back gardens, past allotments and small derelict factories; out to the farthest tip of the most recently constructed tentacle of the London Transport system, Wallingford Bridge, a brand new station built to accommodate the brand new University of Middlesex.

The overhead street lamps were glowing orange in the dusk, and there was a powdering of snow on the pavement as Mr Behrens carried his battered suitcase out of the station, up the long slope which led to the High Street. As he reached it, he became conscious that something was happening.

A group of people was marching down the middle of the road. Most of them were singing or shouting. A lot of traffic had piled up behind them. As they approached, Mr Behrens was able to make out some of the words. The battle cry was "Stoo—dent—Rep—res—en—TAY—shun." One group of hirsute singers was giving a rendering of John Brown's Body, with a chorus of "We won't shave until we get it." A second, rather larger group, was putting over "We'll hang Jack Harraway on a sour apple tree." The only people neither singing nor shouting were the policemen marching beside the leaders.

There were three people in the front rank, and Mr Behrens was able to see them clearly as they walked past. In the middle strode a thickset, red-faced young bull. Sixteen stone of muscle and intolerance. On his right, a thin, coffee-coloured youth with black hair, a hairline black moustache and an appearance of serious gravity. On his left, and thus closest to where Mr Behrens was standing, a girl with a white face and a head of copper curls. Even under the neon lighting, which was being unkind to her colour scheme, she made a striking figure.

Mr Behrens stood watching, until the noise and shouting had faded into the distance, and the last frustrated motorist had ground past. Then he continued on his way. It had started to snow again.

Anyone, he thought, to whom the word "University" still conjured up visions of mellowed stone, creeper-covered walls and smooth lawns would have been in for a shock when confronted with the University of Middlesex. Particularly if the confrontation took place at dusk under a lowering sky. The buildings were not only raw, but seemed to have been designed on an over-ambitious plan, modified from motives of economy, and replanned in a hurry. The general effect was something between a council estate and an army cantonment.

He located the Rector's Lodge at the far end of this conglomeration and was welcomed by the Rector, Dr Harraway, a plump, white-haired man with a professionally ready smile. He said, "Come in, come in. You look frozen. You had to walk? This shortage of taxis is a scandal. An absolute scandal. It's Behrens, isn't it? I'm so glad you've been able to join the faculty as a temporary member. At such short notice, too. You'll be covering Modern European Social and Economic History. When the Minister recommended you to us—a very warm, personal recommendation, incidentally—he mentioned that you were a linguist as well?"

Mr Behrens said, "I have a smattering of most European languages."

"That should be very useful. Many of the leading authorities in your field are in German. As, of course, you will be aware. Is it too much to hope that you might be considering joining us permanently?"

"That will depend on how I get along with your students. I

passed a number of them when I was on my way here. An army with banners."

"They do demonstrate rather a lot," said Dr Harraway. "What was it about this time?"

"The only slogan I could actually make out was 'Hang Jack Harraway'."

The Rector laughed delightedly. "High spirits. They mean no harm. I must have been hanged in effigy a dozen times since I took over at the beginning of last year. It doesn't worry me a scrap."

"Just so long as they continue to do it in effigy, Rector," said Mr Behrens, and took his leave.

It was two days later that he faced his first class. He was interested to find in it all three of the leaders of the demonstration. He had already discovered something about them. The girl was Alison Varney, daughter of Samuel Varney, the property millionaire. The big Irishman was Patrick Meaghan. His grandfather had helped to hold the Dublin Post Office on Easter Day 1916 and had died in its ruins. The thin boy, as he already knew, was Ahmed bin Akbar bin Suleiman, heir apparent to the Ruler of Ras-al-Daar.

On the supposition that what interested him might also interest his students Mr Behrens had chosen to discourse about conditions in Germany between the Wars. He had dealt with Kurt Eisner and with the provisional government of Hoffman and was starting on Bela Kun's Communist regime when the flame-haired Alison interrupted him. She did it politely enough, holding up her hand, and saying, "Do you mind us interrupting you when we want to ask something?"

"Certainly not," said Mr Behrens. "Why?"

"Oh, some of the lecturers get very shirty if we do."

"I can assure you," said Mr Behrens smoothly, "that an amateur lecturer like myself, and one who is rather out of practice at that, positively welcomes interruptions. It not only gives him a breathing space but ensures that the notes he has prepared will last out the hour."

The laugh that greeted this sally was good-natured.

"It was just this," said Alison. "The period you've been

describing. It must have been pretty ghastly. But we know what it was followed by, and that was Hitler. Do you think that Hitler's sort of rule was better, on balance, than what went before?"

"I think," said Mr Behrens slowly, "that Hitler was an unqualified disaster. For Germany and for the whole Western world."

"Isn't that a judgment you're making from post-war books?" said Ahmed.

"If you mean, is it a judgment I'm making only from books, the answer is 'No'. I can speak from personal experience also."

"You met him?"

"Twice."

"But those would be formal meetings. You could make no judgment from them."

"One was formal. One was informal," said Mr Behrens, evasively. "I saw no occasion on either of them to question the verdict of history. Which brings us back to the point. Anarchy and political chaos are usually followed by dictatorship."

"Is that an invariable rule?" said Ahmed. He sounded interested.

"Not invariable. There are exceptions. In Ireland, for instance, political chaos is normally followed by political chaos."

This roused Patrick Meaghan, as, indeed, it had been intended to do. The rest of the hour passed pleasantly enough.

"Who is this man?" asked Meaghan, yawning prodigiously. The three of them were in Alison's cell-like room, Ahmed and Alison sitting on the bed and Pat Meaghan overflowing the only chair.

"He's taking Morovitz's lectures for the rest of this term," said Alison.

"That must be an improvement, however bad he is."

"I think he's rather sweet. And for God's sake stop yawning, Patrick."

"I feel sleepy."

"You can't feel sleepy at four o'clock in the afternoon. And we've got important matters on the agenda. Item one. Tomorrow's demonstration."

"You are determined it shall be violent," said Ahmed.

"Yes. I am. Non-violence has failed. All we've done so far is to hold up the traffic. We've made no impression on the authorities at all." She gave Ahmed a look which was almost motherly, and said, "There's no need for you to join in if you don't want."

"I shall join with the others."

"You don't sound convinced."

"I'm convinced of the rightness of what we are asking for. Not to be treated as children. To have a say in our own affairs. And I am not afraid of violence—I come from a violent country. Of its six last rulers, four have died by violence. But violence leads to a hardening of attitudes. At the moment, few of us feel any animosity towards the authorities. I feel none. To be violent without being provoked seems to me to be wanton."

Alison sighed. She said, "It's very difficult. We'll give Pat the casting vote." A strangled snore came from the chair. "For God's sake. He's asleep."

Alex Fraser was clearly a tycoon. His office, on the eighth floor of the building overlooking the Thames proclaimed as much. It had close carpeting, comfortable chairs, a desk the size of a tennis court, and, in one corner, a neat scale model of a drilling rig. Mr Fraser's blonde secretary, herself a neat scale model, proclaimed it, too. The only unpretentious thing about the whole set-up was Alex Fraser himself. He was small, had a nut-brown face crowned by a mop of greying hair, and was wearing a suit which must have been ten years old at least, and far from well looked after. Mr Calder took in these points at a glance. Being himself a man who disliked pretension, he was prepared, on balance, to disregard the tycoonery and approve of the person.

"It's a damned serious situation," said Mr Fraser. "East Gulf Oil Company, which is one of our subsidiaries, has been working a number of concessions down near Muscat and Oman. They're very promising. And the most promising survey report I've ever read in my life is the one we've just completed in Ras-al-Daar."

"Congratulations."

"Congratulations would be premature. What we had was an exploration contract. Not a drilling contract. That has still to be signed."

Mr Calder said, "Ras-al-Daar? That's old Sheik Akbar. I used to know him quite well. He never struck me as being unduly greedy."

"He's not greedy. He's a desert Arab of the old stock. And he's got ideals. He's seen what money has done to other small Arab States."

"Instant Western civilisation. A package deal, available overnight," said Mr Calder with a shudder.

"It's not all bad. He realises that. The oil revenues will pay for hospitals and roads and education. It'll also bring in alcohol and traffic accidents and the quick-money boys. And jealousy from any neighbour who isn't lucky enough to possess oil. And unrest for his own subjects."

"Not a very attractive balance sheet?"

"Well, maybe I've falsified it a bit. Anyway, that's what the old man's thinking about. And to find out how Western civilisation is working out in practice, he's sent his son to an English University. The F.O. recommended Middlesex. Being new they thought it might be less troublesome."

"They may be new, but they're learning fast. Two days ago they heaved a couple of bricks through the Rector's window. I understand that the change in the Rector's outlook was positively startling. He stopped being a genial uncle or elder brother and became a roaring lion."

"It's wonderful what a well-placed brick will do," said Mr Fraser. "I only hope the thrower wasn't Ahmed?"

"Ahmed was in the forefront of the battle. Mercifully he wasn't pulled in. The police had all their work cut out arresting a wild Irishman. But there's no saying he won't be in trouble next time. And if he spends one night inside an English gaol, your chances in the Eastern Gulf will look a bit sketchy."

Fraser got up, moved across to the corner of the room, and stared malevolently at the model oil rig. He said, "I don't suppose I need explain to you, Calder, just *how* valuable a good concession in that part of the world would be to us right now."

"You don't need to explain," said Mr Calder. "We're taking it seriously all right. My chief, Mr Fortescue, sent a colleague of mine, Mr Behrens, down there at the beginning of term to keep an eye on things. Now he wants me to go down and lend a hand too. Normally Behrens would have been perfectly capable of dealing with a situation like this on his own. But there's a complication."

"What sort of complication?"

"This one's got auburn hair and her name is Alison Varney."

"Sam Varney's daughter?"

"That's right."

"It was bad enough without that," said Fraser, gloomily.

Mr Behrens said, "There's the bell for lunch. Enough tuition for this morning. We'll knock off, shall we?"

Alison Varney shuffled her books and papers into a pile on Mr Behrens' table, sighed, and said, "I'm not really hungry. How could anyone be, the food they serve up here."

Mr Behrens was busy filling his pipe. He said, "Eating's a thing you either worry about a great deal, or not at all. I'm in the second category. When I'm at home, I'm cooked for by my aunt. She permutates on three dishes. Mince, chicken casserole and Irish stew." He had the pipe going nicely now. He added, between puffs, "I've got so little sense of taste that I find them indistinguishable."

Alison said, "Tell me something, Mr Behrens. What are you doing here?"

"Endeavouring to lecture in Social and Economic History."

"Come off it. You're not a don."

"What makes you think that?"

"You don't look like one. Or talk like one. Or think like one."

"You've made a study of the species?"

"Indeed yes. This is the third University I've been to. I was sent down from the other two. For violent and subversive behaviour."

"Did they know that when they accepted you here?"

"Yes. But my father promised them a handsome grant to finish the library."

"I see."

"Do tell. You're some kind of official. An Inspector?"

"Oh dear," said Mr Behrens. "Am I such an obvious civil servant?"

"Or are you something more exciting than that? I have it. You're a member of M.I.5. Come down to spy on us."

Mr Behrens swallowed a mouthful of smoke and started to splutter. Alison patted him on the back, and said, "Own up."

"Since you have guessed half the truth," said Mr Behrens, "I'll tell you the whole. I was planning to take you into my confidence anyway. I've been sent down here to keep an eye on Ahmed, and see he isn't led astray by wild companions."

"Meaning Patrick and me."

"Yes."

"And how were you aiming to do it?"

"I've often found that in a tricky situation the best plan is to co-opt your opponents on to your own side."

"Cool. Tell me more."

"Ahmed's father is hereditary ruler of a patch of desert in the South East corner of the Gulf. It's rather smaller than the Isle of Wight, has a population of nomad Arabs who live by date growing and camel-farming with a side line in gold smuggling. Additionally, it looks like being the brightest prospect for oil that's been turned up for many a year. It would do us a power of good if we were allowed to develop it. Normally, we should be. We discovered it. And we're first in the field for a concession. But if Ahmed gets slung out of an English University or into an English gaol, our prospects will be dim."

"And you're suggesting that I should tell him to be a good boy so that an oil company can make some money."

"Not an oil company," said Mr Behrens. "England."

"Don't tell me you're going to start beating the patriotic drum. Rule Britannia. The Army, the Navy and the Air Force."

"Yes, indeed. And since you mention it, the Air Force in particular. It's amazing to think that thirty years ago there really *were* young men, who grew huge moustaches, and said things like 'Bang on' and 'Wizard prang' and fought their private battles five miles above the fields of Kent, and were burned to death, quite a lot of them, big moustaches and all. And when they knew they were dying, weren't entirely unhappy, because they were doing it for England. Does that make you laugh?"

In the silence that followed, Mr Behrens could hear the distant trampling of feet down the corridors and the banging of doors.

Alison said, "I'm not sure. It's the sort of thing that either makes you laugh or cry. It depends how you look at it. But the point is that it's an anachronism."

"If you mean that we're never going to have another conventional war, I agree with you. More's the pity, I sometimes think."

"Do you mean you *want* another war?"

"It wouldn't affect me. I'm too old. It's the young people I'm thinking about. Fancy living your whole life without ever having a cause worth dying for. Maybe that's what makes them so discontented."

"We have got a cause."

"Breaking the Rector's windows."

"You say that because you don't understand. He can mend his windows. He can't mend his public image."

"What's wrong with his public image?"

"It's a fraud. These places are selling second-class goods. Not even second-class. Shoddy third-class. But it's such a seller's market for Universities just now that they can get away with it. The teaching's a farce. Most of the students could get on faster if they sat at home and read the set books. The brighter ones do."

"You can't manufacture dons overnight."

"Agreed. But what about the living conditions. One bathroom for forty students. When it works. Rabbit hutch cubicles with walls so thin you can hear people talking three rooms away. And the food! If you served up muck like that at Dartmoor you'd have a mutiny."

"And how would you improve it?"

"Simple. Hand over all administrative arrangements to a

committee of students. Do you realise that we've got men here who'd be helping to run businesses if they weren't at University? Women who'd be married, keeping house, maybe looking after a couple of children? And they treat us as though we were children ourselves. That's what we're fighting against. And we're going to go on fighting. I don't suppose any of us will be killed. But we'll be uncomfortable, and some of us will be hurt."

"Suppose I were to agree," said Mr Behrens, "that every word you've said is true. I think you've exaggerated it, but suppose it is true. Must Ahmed be one of the rebels?"

"He and Pat Meaghan are the leaders. Pat's in gaol. If Ahmed backed out, we'd have to start all over again."

"You underrate yourself. They're not the leaders. You are."

"Even if that was true," said Alison, seriously, "I'm not prepared to go on alone."

"You realise that if you go on at all, you're heading for real trouble. Few people fight dirtier than an aroused Establishment."

"If it's going to be a tough and dirty fight, we need a tough and dirty leader. Would you care to take on the job? I'm sure you'd be beautifully unscrupulous. What about it?"

Mr Behrens sighed. He said, "I'm not involved in this fight."

"But you'd enjoy it, wouldn't you? Do you know *when* I spotted that you were different from the rest of the professors? It was when you were talking about Hitler. It's true, isn't it? You did meet him?"

"Yes."

"When?"

"It was in Russia," said Mr Behrens. "In 1943. He made me a personal presentation of the Dresdener Kreuz with crossed palm leaves. I don't think he'd have done it if he'd known that my reason for being there was to arrange for an explosive device to be placed in his private aeroplane."

"There you are," said Alison. "What did I say? You're just the man we need to run a student riot."

Mr Calder sat in the Saloon Bar of the Duke of Pomfret public house in a back street of Wallingford. Thickset, middle-aged, nondescript in appearance and dress, he attracted no attention and desired to attract none.

The snow had changed to frozen rain. The bar was warm and crowded. Mr Calder sipped his whisky and cast an occasional glance at the small serving hatch, through which he could see most of the public bar.

The stout man he was following was sitting in a corner by himself, spinning out half a pint of beer and occasionally glancing at his watch. It was getting on for nine o'clock before the second man joined him. This was a small, spruce character with the look of a prosperous jockey. He carried his drink over and the two men talked for a few minutes. When the packet was passed it was done so inconspicuously that if Mr Calder had not been watching very closely he would have missed it.

Soon afterwards the stout man lumbered to his feet, wrapped a scarf round his neck, said a general "Goodnight" to the bar, and made his way into the darkness of the street. With his head bent forward against the stinging rain he was unaware of anyone behind him until Mr Calder put one hand on his shoulder. As he swung round, Mr Calder clipped him scientifically on the side of the throat, caught him as he fell, gasping for breath, and lowered him gently to the ground. He found the packet in a coat pocket and transferred it to his own. By the time he had done this the stout man was already recovering. Mr Calder helped him up into a sitting position with his back against the railings and said, "If I were you, Mr Ponting, I should go straight home now. You'll get a nasty cold if you sit about in this weather."

"Who exactly *is* Mr Ponting?" said Mr Behrens two days later.

"He keeps a small tobacconists and sweet shop," said Mr Calder. "It's just behind the University and he has a lot of student customers. I'm afraid he sells them nastier things than cigarettes and sweets."

"Cannabis?"

"Yes."

"Hard stuff?"

"I don't think he's got round to it. At the moment, he's strictly on the amateur pot-line. It was because I recognised one of the carriers, a nasty little man called Jacko Simpson—that I was able to get on to him so quickly."

"Bad," said Behrens. "But not too bad yet. What are the authorities going to do about it?"

"It depends what line the Rector decides to take. Ponting, who has about as much courage as a small mouse, tried to buy himself out of the worst of the mess by identifying six students who had had stuff from him. My advice to the Rector was to let me throw a scare into Ponting which would shut him up for good, whilst he gives the students concerned the dressing down of their young lives."

"Will he do it?"

"The snag is that most of them have been in the forefront of the trouble. And one of them is Pat Meaghan."

"He's a vindictive beast," said Mr Behrens. "He won't pass up a chance like this."

"Yes, Miss Varney?" said the Rector, managing to combine in his tones hostility towards a known rebel and a degree of warmth appropriate to the daughter of a possible benefactor.

"It's about Pat Meaghan and the others."

"Which others?"

"The ones who've been buying cannabis, silly young asses."

"I should have used a stronger term myself," said the Rector. "What they have done happens to be a criminal offence."

"Only if you make it so," said Alison. "I gather the police will only push it if you make them."

"Might I ask exactly how you have—er—gathered any of this, Miss Varney. So far as I was aware the whole matter was, at the moment, entirely confidential between myself and the Home Office man who unearthed this scandalous state of affairs."

"These things get about," said Alison, evasively. "The point is, are you prepared to do a deal?"

"A deal?"

"If you'll persuade the police to back-pedal on these charges, I'll guarantee you'll have no more trouble at the College. At least, as long as I'm here."

The Rector had gone very red. He said, "Do you imagine that I could contemplate an outrageous bargain of that sort?"

"I don't suppose you want a lot of trouble when the Minister comes down to open the Library wing next week, do you? He might get the idea that you weren't doing a very good job."

"I fear you misjudge me," said the Rector. His mouth was so tight that the words would hardly come out. "If I had been in any doubt before as to my proper course, this impudent attempt at blackmail and bribery would have made my mind up for me. Now, if you'll excuse me, I have a great many things to do."

"We're on a collision course," said Mr Behrens.

"She sounds a remarkable girl," said Mr Calder.

They were taking tea in the Palm Court of the hotel where Mr Calder was staying. A string quartet was playing selections from the Arcadians.

"Oh, she is. An arresting personality. Her father's a millionaire. She's a dedicated radical extremist. But with a lot more brains than that sort of person usually has. Make *her* Rector, and you'd have a University worth talking about."

"It sounds to me as if you've fallen for her."

"I have," said Mr Behrens. "Hook, line and sinker. Incidentally, she placed me without any difficulty."

"The devil she did. What happened?"

"She offered to withdraw Ahmed from the leadership of the Student Protest Group, on conditions."

"Which were?"

"That I took his place. Even to achieve our main objective I didn't feel able to agree to that."

The Arcadians was inducing a mood of nostalgia in Mr Behrens. They were playing one of the catchy tunes from the second act. *"It's nice and fine. I think that we shall have a lovely day—Eighty in the shade they say—very, very warm for May."* Mr Behrens was humming the words to himself when he realised that Mr Calder had said something.

"What's that about Ahmed?"

"I said, you won't have to bother about Ahmed. His father's ordered him to come home."

"Ordered him home?"

"Nothing to do with the University. The decision was taken on grounds of policy."

"When did you hear?"

"About an hour ago."

"Policy? What policy? Look here, something's up. Why wasn't I told?"

"I've been trying to make up my mind," said Mr Calder, calmly. "Whether I'd tell you at all. Since it's going to make you very angry, I thought I'd let you finish your tea before I did so."

"First we lose Pat, and most of the out-and-outers with him. *They* daren't move hand or foot until the Court case is decided. And now Ahmed. Damn, damn, damn, damn, damn."

It was the first time that Mr Behrens had seen Alison near to tears. He said, "I think it's time I gave you my well-known lecture on tactics. You made a mistake in offering the Rector terms. Never do that when your opponent thinks he's winning. The time for offering terms is when *you're* winning."

"I'm sorry. I don't see—"

"When you have suffered a series of set-backs, when your front is pushed in, your flanks are under fire and your rear is threatened, there's only one thing to do. You attack. The body of the students are behind you. They all realise that the Rector is behaving vindictively. He's never been more unpopular than at this moment. The Press will be here in force when the Minister comes on Wednesday. You've got a golden opportunity to show the world what you think of him."

"It's all very well talking. Do you realise that almost every effective member of our organisation is out of action. You can't build a new committee in forty-eight-hours."

Mr Behrens seemed not to have heard her. He said, "The speeches will take place in the assembly hall. There is some sort of loft above the dais. The ceiling, I noticed, is wood or plaster board. A trap-door cut at the right point—"

"I could think up a lot of marvellous ideas," said Alison, "if we had the people and the equipment. For one thing, do you realise that the assembly hall is locked at night?"

"I have a friend who happens to be staying in Wallingford," said Mr Behrens. "He has a way with locks. He could also get hold of any equipment, in reason, that you want."

"Why should he help? Why should you, come to that?"

"We're both *very* angry with the Rector," said Mr Behrens, gently. "When we're angry, we like to do something about it."

Mr Fortescue looked over the top of his steel-rimmed glasses and said, in tones of cold disapproval, "Do I gather, Behrens, that you had some hand in this disgraceful episode?"

"I organised it," said Mr Behrens, "with a little help from Calder."

"Suppose you are implicated?"

"Not a chance."

"I'm glad you had that much sense." Mr Fortescue resumed his study of the report. "I see that the newspapers speak of an avalanche of soot descending on the Rector *and* on the Minister."

"It was soot mixed with flour, actually. It gave them a very odd appearance."

"Like the black and white minstrels," said Mr Calder.

"Suppose this girl—Alison Varney—is charged with complicity and gives you away."

"Not a shred of evidence against her. She was seated in the third row of the audience and could not possibly have had any hand in opening the trap."

"She didn't throw tomatoes, either," said Mr Calder.

"Tomatoes?" said Mr Fortescue. "There was no mention in the paper of tomatoes."

"About twenty of the students threw them. Oddly enough, they were students who hadn't been particularly militant before."

Mr Fortescue seemed to be visualising the scene. He said, "Soot, flour *and* tomatoes. The Minister is a man who is rather conscious of his personal dignity. I can't think he was pleased."

"He was far from pleased," said Mr Behrens. "And spent,

I believe, the best part of half an hour telling the Rector exactly what he thought of him, and his lack of control over his students. The betting is strongly in favour of a new Rector being appointed."

"I have noticed," said Mr Fortescue, "that when you speak of the Rector, Behrens, you exhibit a most uncharacteristic spirit of personal vindictiveness."

"You know *how* he got rid of Ahmed?"

"I wasn't exactly clear about it," said Mr Fortescue. "I was so relieved that he had left without embarrassment to ourselves that I didn't enquire too closely into the means."

"The Rector had a message conveyed to Ahmed's father," said Mr Calder, "that his son was in danger of being debauched by a girl of Jewish parentage."

"My personal opinion," said Mr Behrens, "is that he was lucky to get off with soot and tomatoes. He deserved boiling lead."

Mr Fortescue rocked silently on his chair for some seconds. His eyes had a far away look. Then he said, "The experiment was tried, in the early twenties, in a Rectorial election at Aberdeen University. It was not an unqualified success."

THE ANNEX

Miriam Sharman

WITH HIS USUAL care, Richard Fletcher drove his car into the big double garage at the bottom of the garden. He walked down the paved path, admiring, as he invariably did, the colourful profusion of roses, still flourishing in mid-September. The front door of the cottage was closed, an unusual occurrence on a warm, sunny evening. The door led directly into the living-room and, as soon as he stepped inside, he recognised trouble. Before the apprehensive silence was broken, he wondered if the cause was another heart attack. If so, it would be his mother's second and not likely to have left her sitting upright in her armchair, albeit with a strained, exhausted look that distressed and alarmed him.

"She's in the annex," she said flatly. "She's dead. I killed her."

"Marian?" Panic made his voice almost inaudible.

Beatrice Fletcher's grip on her walking stick tightened and she hit the carpeted floor with it impatiently. "Of course not. Your wife's gone to Norwich for the day. Felt like having a look at the Cathedral." She made no attempt to conceal her perpetual disapproval of her daughter-in-law.

"Then who . . .?" Richard was so relieved that, for a fleeting moment, the full significance of his mother's words evaded him. He groped. "Who's in the annex?"

"Your mistress—that little slut."

Richard glanced inquiringly at his sister. Was Mother now mentally ill? Edith's eyes, still surprisingly blue in spite of her forty-three years, stared back at him expressionlessly. Her face was pale, but then it always was. She half-turned away from him with a gesture of contempt.

"Mother, I have no mistress. What are you talking about?" His eyes searched the tired, obstinate face.

Edith crossed to the armchair and stood behind it protectively. "Mother meant what she said. The girl's name was Angela Brown. She was pregnant with your child and she said you'd have to marry her."

Richard studied their serious, tense faces, then walked out of the cottage and along the few yards of pebbled path to the wooden annex. Hesitantly, he opened the creaking door. The chintz curtains were drawn across the small window and, after the day's hot sunshine, the room was stifling. Bracing himself, he crossed to the bed and looked down on the fully-clothed body of a young girl. Her pallid face, framed by short, dark hair, appeared quite peaceful. Her eyes were closed.

"Mother did it with a pillow." Edith, standing in the open doorway behind him, was watching him carefully.

"Mother's sixty-six and that girl's barely in her twenties," he said, quietly. "She just let a frail invalid asphyxiate her—without a struggle?"

Edith shook her head. "Mother offered her tea, but she asked if she could have a drink, she felt so weak. She'd been travelling all morning, and what with the baby . . . Mother gave her a large gin, with orange—to mask the sleeping pills she dissolved in it," she added, slowly. "So there was no struggle."

"If you'd got a doctor right away—" Richard began.

"I didn't dare. He'd have had to send for the police if he couldn't save her." Her words came jerkily. "It happened about three o'clock this afternoon. I was out shopping."

He had seen the girl for himself, but he still didn't believe a word of the weird story. There were too many unanswered questions. "What was Mother doing downstairs at three o'clock?" he demanded sharply. "It's her time for resting."

"I left her propped up in the armchair at her bedroom window, as usual," Edith replied, quietly. "You know she can see the garden, and people passing on their way to and from the beach. That's why she likes it here, she knows so many of them and she waves to them and they to her—"

"Yes, yes, I know all that," Richard broke in impatiently.

Edith ignored the interruption. "The girl came through the garden gate and rang the front doorbell. Mother called to her from the window. The girl said she was looking for you. She seemed so distressed, and yet determined, that Mother decided she'd better talk to her. She asked the girl to come up to her room and help her cope with the stairs." Edith lowered her eyes. "By the time I got back at four o'clock, it was all over." She took a deep breath. "I must say, Richard, it was pretty unnerving. Mother was in her chair in the living-room, looking strained but otherwise no different. She was quite calm when she told me what had happened."

"And Marian?" Richard asked, apprehensively.

"Oh, she suddenly decided after breakfast to go off for the day. Nothing unusual about that," she said drily.

No, indeed, he thought. Marian made her escape from Edith whenever she could. "So she knows nothing of this . . . this charade."

Edith shook her head. "It's no joking matter," she said, bitterly.

"I grant you that. It's also a lot of phony nonsense. I suppose we'll have to leave it to the police to unsort the tangle."

Edith's blue eyes were wary. "The police? So what happens to Mother?"

"She'll have to give up this ridiculous story about having killed the girl. Then perhaps we'll get at the truth."

"She won't go back on her story. Why should she? It couldn't have happened any other way. I can vouch for that."

"Whatever way it happened, it's a bloody marvel she's survived the strain, with her heart in the condition it is."

"Sheer tenacity," Edith murmured. "She'll hang on until this thing is settled, then she'll let go gladly. She's said over and over again to me that she's ready to go."

Richard doubted that. The doctor had told him his mother could live for several years with reasonable care. It was more like a bit of Edith's wishful thinking. They all knew she was to inherit this sea-side cottage.

Edith and her husband, Gregory, and their two boys, Jeremy and Frank, always spent part of their school vacations here. Richard and Marian and their three children, two girls and a boy, joined them for the same period. Hence the need for the annex in the garden, used by two of the boys as a bedroom. The cottage, ideally situated away from the busy main thoroughfare, had a large garden with enough grassy lawn for the youngsters, and the beach was only five minutes' walk. When Edith inherited, these family gatherings would end. There was no love lost between Richard and Edith, who was two years older than he and resented his assumption of seniority in family matters. He had little in common with Gregory, his brother-in-law, who lived in Edith's shadow when he wasn't abroad, as he was now, on one of his frequent lecture tours. Marian and Edith constantly got on each other's nerves. Only Beatrice Fletcher had kept the family together, but even she'd had to yield to the children's demands to be allowed to spend a couple of weeks of the long summer vacation with their own friends.

"I—I suppose you must tell the police?" Edith murmured.

"For heaven's sake!" Richard exclaimed. "How do you suggest we get rid of the body?"

"Well, we've only to get through this weekend, then it's back to town. We haven't used the annex since the children left five days ago. If the girl is found later on, it would look as if some outsider had been making use of the annex—nothing to do with us. Anyone could break in or even find a key to fit. We wouldn't have to explain it, just insist we knew nothing about it."

He eyed her speculatively. "You really think that would work?"

She sighed. "It's worth a try, after all, if it would save Mother. We've got to think of her."

"You think she'd agree to that version? Have you discussed it with her?"

"No, not yet, but she might if you suggested it. You're her darling son," she added spitefully.

They both heard Marian driving her car into the garage at the same instant, and they turned and waited for her to come down the garden towards the cottage. Tall and dark, and dressed as usual in strong, gay colours that set off her black hair and grey eyes and clear complexion, she caught sight of them and waved, but her step lost its spring as she drew closer to them.

Thank God she wasn't the helpless, clinging type, Richard

thought. He didn't relish telling her what had happened, but at least he wouldn't have to wrap it up and pretend it was less of a catastrophe than it really was.

"What's wrong, what's the matter?" Marian asked sharply.

Edith began to walk away. "I'll leave you two together," she said. "And I'll get Mother upstairs to bed if I can."

Blocking the entrance to the annex, Richard told his wife what had happened.

"The tigress, protecting her young," Marian murmured.

"You believe Mother's story then?"

"It's in character for her to do such a thing," she said resignedly.

He looked at her curiously. "And it's in character for me to get a young girl pregnant?" he queried.

"I didn't say that," Marian replied, too quickly.

There was a short silence. The lost, unhappy look in her eyes angered him.

"There's a dead girl in there, but I admit I'm more concerned about our relationship at the moment than her violent end. Before we go any further, before I talk to Mother and the police, and try to make some sort of sense of all this, I mean to get things straight between you and me. Now, Marian . . ." She took a step toward him, making a gesture of reconciliation, but he stepped back. "No, not yet. Problems aren't solved on a wave of emotion. Have I been deceiving you with that young girl in there?"

Marian licked her lips. "Don't be so self-righteous, Richard," she said, shakily. "I don't want to believe it, of course." She regained some of her composure and spoke in her natural voice. "But people really are unpredictable, aren't they? We've said so, many times, when we've been discussing others." She smiled a little. "Always other people, of course. But, really, Richard, why not you?"

"Or you?" he asked quietly.

Her smile widened. "You'll have to take my word for it, my dear. I haven't got a lover."

He felt able to smile too. "Nor have I, nor have I had, since we've been married."

Tension eased. The dangerous moment had passed.

Marian insisted on looking at the girl. "Are you sure she's dead?" She peered closely at the inert face. "I've never actually seen a dead body," she murmured.

Richard frowned. "I saw my father, or at least his face, but only for a few moments; you know how it is."

"Yes." Marian's hand hovered over the girl's forehead, then she touched it tentatively. "She's so . . . so still. One feels for a pulse, I think."

Richard watched with mixed feelings as she fumbled with the girl's wrist. Marian shook her head. "I can't feel anything." Her voice was strained. "Richard, would you . . . could you listen . . . for a heartbeat?"

He gestured her aside, leaned over the motionless body, and let his ear rest on the girl's chest. "It's hopeless." He straightened. "She's been like this for nearly four hours," he pointed out.

"Your mother must know, Richard. After all, she was a qualified nurse." She giggled. "Something nasty in the woodshed . . ."

He was saved from facing up to the implications of his mother's medical knowledge by the unexpected crack in Marian's self-control.

"Stop it, Marian," he snapped.

She took a deep breath. "I'm all right, really." Richard released her and she stepped back, frowning, puzzled. "I've seen her, somewhere. Richard, I know her face." Her voice trailed off. "But I can't place her."

Richard's momentary surprise gave way to indifference. "We know her name. There's no mystery."

"If only I could remember. It's so silly," Marian muttered, "but it keeps happening, doesn't it? One sees a face that's somehow familiar . . ."

"We'd better go back to the cottage," Richard said, leading the way. As they entered, they heard Edith's firm footsteps coming down the steep, narrow staircase. Her pale face looked grey in the evening sunlight that filtered through the living-room window.

"How's Mother?" Richard demanded.

She shook her head. "Poorly. We'll have to fix up a bed in here. Those stairs are impossible for her."

"But she's always refused to turn this room into a bedroom," Marian protested.

Richard sighed. Usually decisive, quick to react, not easily sidetracked, he was at a loss to know how to deal with the incredible situation. His lawyer's mind tried to examine detachedly what at the moment passed for evidence, but emotional involvement kept getting in the way. He disliked and distrusted his sister. On the other hand, as he was devoted to his mother, he could not bring himself to accept her version of the girl's violent death. The obvious thing to do was to call the police, and the longer he delayed the more risky it would be.

"I'm going up to talk to Mother," he said abruptly.

Beatrice Fletcher lay propped up on her pillows, her white, exhausted face slack and still. She opened her faded eyes and smiled at him, a faint, forced smile which she couldn't maintain.

He pulled up a chair and took her chill, dry hand in his. "How do you feel?" he asked softly.

"Weak," she said. "I don't want to talk, Richard."

She was very ill, he acknowledged, but she was putting on some of this helplessness, he felt sure. She had borne her illness indomitably but she had also used it with remarkable skill to continue to get her own way whenever the occasion had arisen. Richard was aware of this and rather admired her for it. She tightened her thin lips and sank her chin into her chest.

"That girl wasn't my mistress but even if she claimed to be, I can't believe you killed her—just for that. Why did you?" he asked.

"Not for you, nor for Marian, but for the children. Someone had to think of them." Her voice was weak but the words came clearly enough.

"But a murder trial—where everything is bound to come out—that's not much protection for the children."

A faint smile softened the haggard face and she opened her eyes, resting them on her son's worried face. "There will be no trial, no publicity. Call the police, Richard, now. I want to make a statement." She sighed. "Then I can let go. I'm tired, so tired."

He still didn't believe her but the police probably would. They didn't know his mother like he did, they would accept her motive. That meant his character being blackened, and perhaps gossip would leak out, not at all a nice prospect. Suddenly he realised she was staring at him intently.

"Don't worry, Richard, about your own image. You don't live here, your home's far away. It doesn't matter about local gossip. And you won't come back here when I'm gone."

"Mother, I can't let you do this for Edith."

Her eyes flickered angrily. "Edith . . . Edith's vulnerable . . . a mother . . . Gregory's useless." She broke off. "How did you know?"

"I couldn't see you killing anyone in cold blood. It had to be Edith."

He couldn't understand her reaction—a bitter smile, a sigh of impatience. "You're wrong, Richard. I could and I did."

He bent down and brushed her forehead with his lips. "Have it your own way, Mother," he said quietly, and was rewarded with the look of relief that crossed her face.

In the living-room, Edith and Marian waited for him, each preoccupied with her own thoughts.

"I can't shake her story," he said, "and I'm sure the police won't."

"Why should you, or they, want to?" Edith asked sharply. "Why should she take the blame if she hadn't done it?"

He looked at her speculatively. "I'm just as curious as the police are going to be, Edith, as to how Mother got the girl into the annex."

"After they'd talked for a little while in here, Mother asked her to wait in the annex as the cottage was like a hotel, with people dropping in all the time," Edith explained patiently. "Then Mother took the drink to her in the annex. The girl grumbled about feeling tired, so Mother told her to stretch out on the bed—" She broke off, and there was a long, brittle silence.

The conversation he'd just had with his mother nagged at

Richard's mind. For a moment they had been talking at cross-purposes. She'd thought his reference to Edith had been about something else.

"Why didn't you call the doctor?" he asked, returning to the attack.

"I told you, I didn't dare." She half-turned away, avoiding his eyes. "Anyway, Mother insisted on no doctor, and one doesn't defy her, Richard, in the state she's in." She faced them again, suddenly angry. "You think I killed that girl, don't you, both of you?"

"Listen, Edith," Richard said quietly, "as I am the only one who knows with absolute certainty that the dead girl was not my mistress, I find Mother's motive utterly bewildering."

"That was what the girl told her," Edith replied irritably. "I can understand your denying it but, all the same, it's what Mother believed. Look, Richard, Mother's no fool and there's nothing wrong with her mind. All the circumstantial details of her story will be checked: the time of the girl's arrival—somebody's sure to have seen her—and my shopping alibi. When they've established the time of death, they'll know I couldn't have done it." She spoke defiantly, but confidently.

"You don't believe me when I tell you the girl was not my mistress?"

She lowered her eyes. "You don't believe me when I tell you I didn't kill her." Her lips trembled. "After all, murder is somewhat worse than . . . than infidelity." She crossed quickly to the staircase. "I'm going up to sit with Mother for a while."

Richard threw up his hands in despair and turned to Marian. "What a mess, what a bloody mess," he muttered. "I can't bring myself to telephone the police. I just don't believe Mother callously murdered that young girl."

"I believe it, Richard," Marian said calmly, "because I'm not emotionally involved, as you are."

His eyes clouded. "You know I've never been sloppy about Mother," he protested. "I've always acknowledged her faults."

"Yes, yes," she said impatiently. "Little human weaknesses, like we all have. Small deceits to get her own way, that sort of thing. But to me, she's a ruthless, self-righteous woman."

He thought this over for a few moments. "But you can't be sure. There's Edith—"

"You dislike Edith," Marian said quietly.

"I take your point. All the same, Marian—" His mouth tightened into the familiar, obstinate Fletcher line. "Mother's not capable of deliberate murder."

There was no sense in arguing, Marian knew. She spoke placatingly. "When the police come, you mustn't dispute your mother's motive, otherwise the whole thing collapses. There will be too much investigation and heaven knows where that will lead to."

Richard eyed her warily. "You mean you want me to admit this girl was my mistress even though you don't believe it yourself?"

Marian nodded. "After your mother's given the police her statement, she might tell *us* the truth."

"Yes, you're right, she probably will." his hand hovered over the telephone.

"Richard, wait a minute." Marian's voice sounded urgent. "You're tired, and Edith's had a terrible day. Leave it till the morning."

"But the longer we delay—" he began.

"We can fix the time of your mother's confession to us to suit ourselves."

"True . . ." He needed no more persuasion. "And I'd like to be thinking clearly. I'll have to provide some convincing background, I suppose, to my love life with this girl. I'm sure Edith and Mother will see the advantage of leaving it till morning."

That night, he tossed fitfully and restlessly for over two hours. Eventually, a double dose of sleeping pills took effect and he dropped off into an exhausted sleep.

Marian had forced herself to stay awake, waiting for this moment. She wrapped herself in a warm dressing gown and went quietly downstairs. The familiarity of the girl's face had kept nagging at her mind. Vaguely, irrationally, she felt that if she could only identify her, it would somehow help them out of their impasse. She didn't examine the idea too closely. She just felt she must have another look at the girl, in the undisturbed quiet of the night. It was a spooky thing to do, she acknowledged to herself, but she'd just have to face it.

She'd had to hide her intention from Richard. He wouldn't have tried to prevent her but he'd have insisted on accompanying her, distracting her, when she needed all the concentration she could muster. By the light of the torch she made her way cautiously across the moonless garden to the annex. She hesitated, her hand on the latch, swallowed her revulsion, and opened the door slowly. The slight creak sounded in her ears like a pistol shot and she held her breath; then she realized nobody in the house could possibly have heard it.

She masked the strong light from the torch with her hand, moved toward the bed, the girl's figure in outline coming into view as she drew nearer. Then she froze. For a moment, sheer terror took over.

The girl was now lying half on her side, her legs curled up slightly. Someone had moved her, Marian thought wildly, but why! She forced herself to hold the torchlight on the girl's face. It was still pale but no longer stark. The girl was alive. With her knees almost turning to water and her whole body trembling with shock and, above all, relief, Marian sat down on the chair by the bedside and let her tears flow.

The girl stirred and opened her eyes with difficulty. To Marian she looked more familiar than ever, the large, lovely dark eyes, at the moment misted by drowsiness or whatever it was that had brought her so close to death. She blinked two or three times, then won the struggle for wakefulness. It took some effort to get out the words: "I feel bloody awful."

Marian dabbed her face and hoped the tears wouldn't show, then switched on the bedside lamp. The girl quickly closed her eyes as if unable to bear the sudden light.

"Oh, I'm sorry—" Marian began.

"Leave it, I'll get used to it," but she kept her eyes shut. "My mouth—I feel as if I've been chewing gravel."

The well-spoken, modulated voice surprised Marian. Without spelling it out to herself, she had felt that the girl must be a pathetic deprived member of the lower classes. Perhaps her clothes had given that impression. They were of the fashionable sort worn by the young nowadays, cheap and flamboyant. Her hands, however, were immaculate, with over-manicured nails. She drew herself up on to one elbow, opened her eyes, and stared at Marian. "What time is it?" she asked.

"It's nearly four o'clock . . . in the morning."

The girl blinked. "In the morning," she repeated, her voice almost drying up.

Marian poured her a glass of water from the carafe. She sipped it slowly at first, then drained the glass, A little colour returned to her face and the glazed look in her eyes faded a little. "Do you mean to say I've slept here since . . . since about three o'clock this . . . no, yesterday afternoon?" She frowned. "There's been some funny business. That old girl was a bit too good to be true." Suspicion and hostility took over. "And who are you? And what are you doing, sitting at my bedside at this hour?" She looked appraisingly at Marian. "I'm strictly heterosexual." She patted her abdomen. "Is Jeremy around?"

Jeremy! Jeremy's interest in the television studio near his school was a family joke. The elusive fragments crystallized in Marian's mind. She had seen Angela Brown on television, in very small dramatic parts.

"Jeremy's camping in France with some other boys until he goes back to college in a few weeks," Marian replied carefully.

"Oh, yes, I know all that. But I thought I'd catch him before he left." She pushed herself up, leaned for a moment against the pillows, then sat up, her strength increasing with each moment that passed. A pillow lying at the foot of the bed caught her eye and she studied it with a puzzled frown. "I don't remember that being there. . . ." She paused. "But there's something, I can't quite . . ." She sighed. "Oh well, I daresay it will all come back when I've had some nourishment."

The soft, fuzzy expression had cleared, revealing a hard and wary pair of eyes.

"Do you feel well enough to come across to the house?" Marian asked stiffly.

"I bloody well do, I'm ravenous. And if Jeremy's not here, someone's got to listen to me."

She was a little unsteady on her feet and was glad of Marian's helping arm. So, it was Jeremy, Marian thought, as they crossed the garden with the help of the torch; Jeremy and not Richard. She had believed Richard, of course, but it was bliss to have it confirmed.

She hurriedly made some ham sandwiches and a large pot of strong, black coffee, and while Angela was eating and drinking, she went upstairs, shook Richard out of his drugged sleep with a hurried explanation. There was no need to waken Edith. She appeared on the landing, demanding to know what was going on.

They joined the girl in the living-room. Edith stared at her as if hypnotized. Angela stared back.

"You're Jeremy's mother," she said. "He's shown me snaps. He's a bit like you—those blue, blue eyes . . ." She shrugged. "I'm Angela Brown." She eyed Richard appreciatively. "Uncle Richard, I presume?"

He turned and looked helplessly at Marian. "Where do we begin?" he asked.

Edith's voice was hard. "She came here to browbeat Jeremy into marriage, to ruin his life . . .".

Angela's laugh came spontaneously. "You must be joking! Jeremy's been doing the browbeating. I just want to get rid of this." She patted her abdomen again. "I don't want to marry him. I thought I'd catch him before he left for France."

"You're lying! You must be," Edith said, "or why did my mother . . ." She let the words hang in the air. There was a moment's brittle silence. Angela looked from one to the other, pursing her expressive mouth. Nobody completed Edith's question.

"Look, this is getting boring," the girl said. "I told the old lady I'd come to ask Jeremy to marry me because I thought that was the best way to handle her. She was very calm and reasonable, so I thought the best way to play it was in the role of the *ingénue*—bewildered, seduced by her darling grandson —looking for help from her beloved's family. I hadn't really rehearsed it that way but when I realised Jeremy wasn't here, I decided to start off on the innocent maiden role and play it by ear after that."

"You didn't fool her," Richard said, quietly. "She called you a slut."

"Pooh! Words like that . . ." She snapped her fingers.

Richard poured himself a cup of coffee and sipped it quickly, in the hope that it would clear his mind and help him shake off his hangover from the sleeping pills. Barbiturates always left him thickheaded. He turned away from the girl and spoke directly to Edith. "Mother must be told," he said.

"When she wakens naturally," Edith said. "Not before." She made a gesture of distaste towards Angela. "And certainly not until we've got rid of her." She spoke directly to the girl. "I'll give you four hundred pounds for your abortion," she said.

"Six hundred," Angela replied promptly. "I'll need a bit of a holiday after it."

"How can I be sure you'll leave Jeremy alone?"

Angela made a rude gesture. "If you believe I'm after your darling boy," she said contemptuously, "you'll believe anything. I've got a big career ahead of me. I'm a good actress and I'm going to be a great one. I don't want anything else. I left home because my parents opposed my going to drama school. They wanted me to go to college. So I simply walked out on them and took the first bit part I could get. I've got to fight my way up in that rat race with what talents I've got, understand? Marriage to Jeremy would be the end." She emphasised her words with an admonishing finger waved at Edith. "You ought to know your own son. He's a gooey romantic. Wants to marry me, wants me to have the baby, wants me to live in an apartment with him while he finishes school. She drained her coffee cup. "He's nothing but a bore, I tell you," she said mildly. "A dreary bore."

Edith was shaking with humiliation, humiliation that this detestable girl could reject her son. "You're sure the baby's Jeremy's?" she demanded.

Angela whirled on her. "No! I'm not sure. Do you want to make something of that?"

For a moment it looked as if Edith would strike her. Her face was flushed and her blue eyes blazed with anger.

"You're lucky to be alive, you cheap little tart," she cried.

"My mother doped your drink with sleeping pills and when you were unconscious, she stuffed a pillow over your mouth, to finish you off. She thinks she killed you! We thought she'd killed you!"

Recollection dawned slowly on Angela's face. "I was nearly out, but not quite. I held my breath. She was feeble, really, that's what I remember thinking." Her large dark eyes widened in horror. "I must have hung on by a thread . . .". She looked around the room at each of them in turn, her contempt almost tangible. "That's great, just great, sitting in moral judgment of me because you don't like my sex life. And that old trout! I'll tell her a thing or two." She dashed across the room and up the staircase.

There was a paralysed silence. Richard faced his moment of truth with bitter resentment. He'd better try to stop the confrontation, he decided, but when he reached the landing, Angela was already at his mother's door. He stood quite still and watched her as she pushed it open. The dawn light was filtering through the curtains and the girl stood, framed in the open doorway, like an avenging angel.

"Ghost . . ." He heard his mother's voice choke on the word.

Unhurriedly, he crossed to the bedside. This time he knew with certainty, and with relief, that he was looking at death.

MRS CRAGGS AND THE LORDS SPIRITUAL AND TEMPORAL

R. F. Keating

IT WAS A funny thing, Mrs Craggs used to say about the cleaning job she once had at the House of Lords, but, in spite of it all being so hoity-toity, there was always a lot of what you might call capers. Nothing nasty, mind. Well, not until That Day. But definitely capers.

Things like the great writing paper row. Between the Bishop of Porchester, that was, and Tryulph, fourteenth Earl Balerno and Gosforth. Well, that was the name that Mr Holofernes, the Attendant whose domain coincided with Mrs Craggs', always used for him. Every time. The whole lot. Mrs Craggs called him Lord Bally Earn Oh. And sometimes to his face. Because he was one of the few peers she ever had many dealings with, seeing that her work in the place—carpets hoovered and surrounds polished, general tidying and everything else dusted and rubbed till it shone—was done in the mornings while their noble lordships did their work—revising Bills sent from the House of Commons, starting up a few quiet Bills of their own and general debating at a high moral level—in the afternoons of Tuesdays, Wednesdays and Thursdays. But Lord Balerno and Gosforth was a particularly sleepy little peer curling up like a rabbit on the red leather benches of the chamber during debates and quite often tucking himself away in a corner and being found only next morning by Mrs Craggs as she went about her work. That was the way she had got to know him.

And an old fuss-pot he was, she used to tell her friend Mrs Milhorne who had charge of the next set of committee rooms at that time—and her polish not a patch on mine, Mrs Craggs used to think, but not say—always on about waste and things not being in their places and people "misusing" this and that.

"Misusing" was a favourite word of his. And "misusing" was what he had accused the Bishop of Porchester of in the great writing paper row.

"Well, of course," Mrs Craggs said to Mrs Milhorne, "that old Lord Spiritual had asked for it. The way he went on."

"Yes," Mrs Milhorne agreed rather doubtfully, "it don't seem right to be so sort of desperate. Well, not for a bishop."

"Desperate," Mrs Craggs replied with a sniff. "Pig-headed's what I call it. Downright pig-headed, he is, that old bish. Why, he'd call black white if he thought it was red, and well you know it."

The Bishop of Porchester, indeed, had been nominated to his see many years before during the full flow of a Labour Government and with the passing of time his opinions had, if anything, become more left-wing than ever. And it had been a very left-wing letter to a newspaper written on House of Lords writing paper which had been the cause of the trouble between himself and the fourteenth Earl Balerno and Gosforth, otherwise Old Bally Earn Oh.

Often, as Mrs Craggs, her day's work done, made her way out through the lofty spaces of St Stephen's Hall—Mr Holofernes, who seldom missed a chance of imparting information of an edifying character, could never refer to the hall without pointing out that it had been behind the statue there of the great Edmund Burke, "that hincomparable horator", that the maniac Bellingham had lurked in the year 1812 before striking down Spencer Perceval, "twenty-first Prime Minister"—she used to say to herself that the old House of Lords was at least always good for a bit of a laugh. It was as nice a job that way as she'd ever had, except for the too often looming presence of Mr Holofernes in his statutory black tail suit with that big gold medallion dangling under his long solemn face and his way of looking down his nose and loosing off "a whole lot of stuff as you'd rather not be put to the trouble o' remembering."

"All the same," Mrs Milhorne would say when Mrs Craggs stated her opinion of Mr Holofernes, "all the same he has give his life to the House. You can't deny that." She would sigh then. A great gusty sigh, from right down in the depths of her soul. "I think I may give my life to something," she would add. "Only, o' course, there's me health."

"Well, this ain't getting no dusting done," Mrs Craggs would quickly bang in then. She had heard a great deal in her time about Mrs Milhorne's health.

Yes, she thought as she set to work putting a bit of good old elbow grease on to the tops of the low cupboards that ran along one wall of Committee Room F, it's all very well giving your life to a place, but that don't entitle you to tell everyone time and again that the Lord Chancellor sits on the Woolsack when presiding over the house but does not "hact in the capacity of chairman, the House conducting its business without a Chair". All standing up, I suppose, Mrs Craggs liked to mutter then. And as for that big red leather pouffe, as she called the Woolsack after she had been taken from her regular duties once to work in the chamber itself, well, what if it was filled with "samples of wool from all parts of the hEmpire"? There hadn't been an empire, not what you could call an empire, for years. And a good job too. High and mightying it over all those poor natives.

Nor did "giving your life" to a place entitle you every time Lord Pinnborough, who was a regular old barrel of lard, came waddling and wheezing by to recall at length that once when Lord Norris and Lord Grey were tellers and Lord Norris "being subject to vapours" was not paying attention Lord Grey had counted a particularly corpulent peer as ten lords and so a Bill had been passed that never should have been. Or, every time the Marquess of Middlehampton came to the House (which was very often) to go on about how that peer—mad as a hatter, he was, Mrs Craggs knew well—had had the distinction of having another peer "move that the clerk at the Table do read the hOrder of the House relating to asperity of speech against him, an event that hoccurs hardly once in your average lifetime".

Mrs Craggs never let all that stop her getting on with her work, even though Mr Holofernes seemed to find plenty of time to stand about loosing off. But then he had a way with the House that was all his own—perhaps because of the life he had given to it—extending right down to what was served in the Lords refreshment rooms. "We have a particularly fine Madeira wine, Mrs C, the like of which, as I can vouch for, you will not find helsewhere".

Yes, there were some capers that went on. And when it came to tidying up of a morning, there were some funny things she'd found lying about too. Once a live hen, "sitting there quiet as you please, clucking away like she owned the place". That had proved to be a notion of waddling old Lord Pinnington's who had wanted to make a point when someone had "moved for papers on the agricultural question", only fellow peers had luckily dissuaded him from actually taking the fowl into the chamber. And often enough there were small paper bags of Nuttall's Mintoes. Those always had to be returned to Lord Middlehampton as quickly as possible before he exploded into one of his rages once again. And another time there had been a Kalashnikov machine rifle, courtesy of the Bishop of Porchester. And not once but twice there had been little wash-leather bags containing a number of gold sovereigns. And no one had ever claimed either of those. But the most surprising thing of all Mrs Craggs ever found was on one Wednesday morning. The Wednesday she ever afterwards thought of as That Day.

She had been delayed by a series of small mishaps and had not managed to get into Committee Room F until about eleven o'clock, when she really should have been already on her way home. So she had scurried round with her preliminary tidying-up. When she had got to the row of low cupboards running all along one wall under a big gloomy picture of one of the Lords Chancellor in voluminous robes and dusty-looking full-bottomed grey wig she had caught a strong whiff of peppermint. Another of his little old bags, she had thought, and had whipped open the sliding door of the cupboard. Only to find Tryulph, fourteenth Earl Balerno and Gosforth. And this time he was not sleeping but very plainly murdered.

What a kerfuffle there had been then. Mrs Craggs had, quick as you like, slammed the cupboard door across again and had gone to look for somebody to break the news to. Unfortunately who should be almost immediately outside the door of

Committee Room F but Mr Holofernes, black tail suit, dangling gold medallion, long solemn face and all. So Mrs Craggs had told him. Which turned out to be a fair mistake. Because Mr Holofernes, having first alluded briefly to the assassination of Spencer Perceval, "twenty-first Prime Minister", took it into his head that the matter would have to be dealt with by the Serjeant-at-Arms and by no one else.

"Get the police," Mrs Craggs said. "Phone the Yard and quick about it. This is murder. Someone's been killed."

"A peer of the realm has been done to—" Mr Holofernes began argumentatively.

"Get the police," said Mrs Craggs.

And Mr Holofernes went then suddenly meek as a lamb to the nearest telephone and dialled 230 1212. And he passed on the message to such effect, too, that in less than a quarter of an hour two gentlemen from Scotland Yard were entering Committee Room F.

By that time, too, of course, various other people had arrived, summoned chiefly by Mr Holofernes, restored again to his customary state of dignity. There was the Serjeant-at-Arms, who was a retired Air Vice-Marshal. There was the Staff Superintendent, who was a retired Naval Lieutenant-Commander. There was the Yeoman Usher of the Black Rod, who was a retired Naval Captain. There was the Gentleman-Usher of the Black Rod, who was a retired Lieutenant-General. And there was—nobody quite knew why—the Examiner of Private Acts, who was a lady barrister of formidable intelligence given to wearing little red hats. And half a dozen other people of much less consequence, including Mrs Craggs and her friend Mrs Milhorne.

"Now then," said the first of the Scotland Yard gentlemen, a tall man with a face almost as lugubrious as that of Mr Holofernes, dressed in a dark blue suit of ferocious respectability. "Now then, where might I find this alleged body? And who might be the person who made the initial discovery?"

And that brought Mrs Craggs, who had been standing near the door wondering whether she ought to slip quietly out and wait somewhere else, to the fore once again. She made her way over to the fatal cupboard.

"It's here, Superintendent," she said, deciding that that exalted rank, read about often enough in her study of juicy murders in the papers, must be about right. "Here, in this old cupboard, Superintendent."

"Sergeant, if you please," said the man with the dark blue suit. "Detective Sergeant Browne."

"Well, it's here then, Sergeant Brown," said Mrs Craggs.

The sergeant crouched down to open the cupboard, turning momentarily to Mrs Craggs as he did so and giving her a somewhat baleful look.

"Browne with a 'e'," he said creakily, as if he was certain that Mrs Craggs had repeated his name without that final enriching, if mute, letter.

And she had.

Sergeant Browne took one quick look into the cupboard, saw what Mrs Craggs had seen earlier and rose to his feet.

He turned to the other Scotland Yard man, whom Mrs Craggs now swiftly transformed into the Detective Superintendent in charge, in spite of his rather undistinguished appearance. He had a snubby button nose and his stripey grey herring-bone suit was shiny at the elbows.

"It's murder right enough, Super," he said. "I'll leave the evidence till the team arrives."

Mrs Craggs did not much like hearing Old Bally Earn Oh called "the evidence". In spite of his infuriating fussiness about such things as the use of House of Lords writing paper, or rather its misuse, she had liked the old boy and had always woken him as gently as she could on the mornings she had found him curled up in a corner. "I wonder if he ever comes to in the middle of the night," Mrs Milhorne had once speculated. "I wouldn't like to wake and find myself in this creepy old place. Think of what he might of seen." Ghosts seemed to be in Mrs Milhorne's mind. But Mrs Craggs had not been able to resist in saying "Yeh. Mice, I shouldn't wonder. Amount of food gets left about." And Mrs Milhorne had given a delicate, breathy shriek.

The Detective Superintendent took Sergeant Browne at his word and at once began establishing who the dead man was, accepting Mrs Craggs' temporary identification without demur, despite an attempt by Mr Holofernes to take this important task upon himself.

"Well now, Mrs Craggs," the Detective Superintendent finished, "I don't think we need you any more just now. But if you'd stay in the building, you'd oblige me. I'll want to see you again shortly. My name's Brown, by the way. Brown. Without an 'e'."

And he gave Mrs Craggs what looked suspiciously like the merest flick of a wink.

So Mrs Craggs went and waited outside and saw all the bustle. The men Sergeant Browne had referred to as "the team" arrived, experts every one, carrying bulky boxes and cameras and tripods and a brown canvas stretcher and trying not to look overawed by their unusually august surroundings. And the Press arrived and were met full face by Mr Holofernes, but stopped in front of him only long enough to hear him "venture to remind you gentlemen of the recent hencounter between Tryulph, fourteenth Earl Balerno and Gosforth, and his Lordship the Bishop of Porchester" before nudging each other crudely in the ribs and sweeping past, eyes intent on the closed door of Committee Room F.

But there they met Sergeant Browne—"with an 'e' if you please, gentlemen, when you come to file your reports"—and found an altogether more formidable obstacle, though they were eventually promised a statement from Detective Superintendent Brown—"without an 'e' as it happens, gentlemen"—in about an hour's time.

Mrs Craggs was standing an hour later near the open door of Committee Room G where the Press Conference was held, talking to Mrs Milhorne, who had not been asked to stay but who thought she should not travel on her own "after the shock". So she chanced to hear most of what the button-nosed Detective Superintendent said. It was not a great deal, however, mostly about "an investigation in its very early stages" and having "reason to believe the case is one of foul play" and "fullest inquiries" and "many lines yet to be followed up". But it was when after this that she overheard one of the departing reporters, a young man with heavy hornrim spectacles and a safari jacket, say "Police Baffled, that's what it amounts to, boys" that she decided that she had a duty which she had to perform.

So she knocked on the now closed Committee Room door and when it was opened by Sergeant Browne said she wanted to see the Detective Superintendent.

"My good woman," said the sergeant, "Detective Superintendent Brown is a very busy man."

"I dare say," said Mrs Craggs. "But I was the one what found the body, you know. And I've got something as I wants to tell him."

"I am aware of your role in the affair," Sergeant Browne replied. "And I have to inform you that in due course we shall require to take your fingerprints. This will be strictly for elimination purposes, and at the end of the inquiry you will have the right to witness their destruction, if so be you so wish."

"And when's the end of the inquiry going to be?" Mrs Craggs asked trenchantly.

"That I am unable to say, though I should estimate that, in the nature of things, a period of some weeks should elapse."

"Would you?" said Mrs Craggs, when she had worked out what all the words meant. "Some weeks, eh? Well, I should estimate that it'll be in the nature o' some minutes."

Sergeant Browne sighed.

"If you have information which you believe may contribute to the successful outcome of our inquiry," he said, and the emphasis he put on "you believe" would have sunk a smallish battleship, "then I suggest you impart the same to me without further delay."

"No," said Mrs Craggs.

"My good woman, either you have something to tell us, in which case you would do well to tell me immediately, or you have not, in which case I would request you not to take up more of my not unvaluable time."

"Yeh," said Mrs Craggs. "And now can I see the Super?"

"You may not."

Mrs Craggs considered for an instant.

"All right," she said, "I'll tell you this much. It's to do with a suspect."

Sergeant Browne looked at her, his face solemn with scepticism.

"I suppose it's the Bishop of Porchester," he said. "Same as your mate Holofernes, or whatever he calls himself, gave us. Very keen to point to the Bishop was Mr Holofernes. Only as it so happens the Bishop was in church at the material time, in front of a congregation of forty-eight mothers of children about to be confirmed."

"I dare say," Mrs Craggs replied unperturbed. "And I might add that mate of mine old Holofernes is not. In fact . . ."

She gave Sergeant Browne a shrewdly assessing look.

"In fact, it was Mr Holofernes as I wanted to talk to you about," she went on. "Things like a certain taste for House of Lords madeira wine. Things like a certain habit of Old Bally—of the late victim of falling asleep in a corner and may be waking up in the middle of night and seeing certain people, whose whole life was in this place, helping themselves to more than what they ought."

In the lugubrious face in front of her a gleam was slowly entering two mournful brown eyes.

"I thought as how I ought to mention it," Mrs Craggs continued. "Specially in view of a certain gentleman what has a dangly gold medallion around his neck being recently seen a-getting into his overcoat."

"Stay there, my good woman," said Sergeant Browne, mournful eyes now glowing like two amber traffic lights. "Stay there and don't move."

And away he went, almost breaking into an undignified run. But not quite.

And, as soon as his blue-suited back had disappeared round the nearest corner, in went Mrs Craggs to Committee Room G, without so much as knocking.

Detective Superintendent Brown did not look altogether pleased to see her.

"Mrs Craggs, isn't it?" he said, looking up from the massive copy of *Debrett's Peerage, Baronetage, Knightage and Companionage* which he had been going through with an expression of fair dismay on his button-nosed face. "I'm afraid I'm rather busy just now, but if you'd care to wait."

"I think I'd better not," Mrs Craggs answered. "You see I got something to tell you, an' I've a feeling I might be stopped by that sergeant of yours if I don't give it you straight away."

Detective Superintendent Brown put a ballpoint as a marker among the many pages of *Debrett.*

"All right," he said, "tell me."

Mrs Craggs drew in a deep breath by way of gathering her thoughts.

"Well," she said, "it's him really. Sergeant Browne, with an 'e'."

The two sharply curious eyes on either side of the button nose went suddenly hard.

"You're not going to tell me Sergeant Browne murdered his lordship, are you?"

"Good lord, no, sir. I mean, why should he ever? No, it's something else about him. Something silly really. But important. If you know what I mean."

"Go on."

"Well, it's this. When he opened that cupboard next door to see if I was round the bend or something and found there really was a murdered body in there, well, he was a bit busy at that moment a-telling me that Browne was spelt with an 'e', and I don't think he noticed something. And o' course by the time all those fellers arrived with their cameras an' all I dare say it's gorn."

"What had gone, Mrs Craggs?"

"Why, the smell. The strong, strong smell o' peppermint there was when I first opened the cupboard and then shoved the door back across, what Sergeant Browne later left open. That was what first made me look in there, you know. The peppermint."

"I see. A strong smell of peppermint. And that tells us something, does it?" Detective Superintendent Brown's undistinguished face was decidely thoughtful. "Or at least it tells you something, I suspect, Mrs Craggs."

"Nuttall's Mintoes," said Mrs Craggs. "That Lord Middlehampton always sucking 'em. Ask anybody. And temper. Terrible. Ask anybody else."

But the person Detective Superintendent Brown, without an 'e', asked was the Marquess of Middlehampton himself. And that Lord Temporal said right out, "Of course I made away with the fellow. Blackguard. He'd stolen something very precious from me. Some Mintoes. Nuttall's Mintoes. The fellow was a disgrace to the House. He had to go. He had to go."

So they took the Marquess of Middlehampton and put him in another sort of house, not quite so distinguished but an equally permanent institution. And Mrs Craggs soon afterwards gave in her notice to the Staff Superintendent because somehow that old House of Lords was not such a place for funny capers any more.

THE NEWTONIAN EGG

Peter Godfrey

"THE DYING MAN," said Hal Brooke, "ate a hearty wedding breakfast."

On the other side of the room Kurtz, also with a tray on his knees, sneered. He said: "It's a funny thing about this disease. You can feel on top of the world one minute, and be knocking at the pearly gates the next. Even if you are getting married this afternoon, you could pop off just as well today as any other day." He grinned. "Maybe the excitement will make it even more likely. You know, I've been thinking about it for the last few minutes—trying to imagine which would be the most appropriate moment for you to kick the bucket. At first I thought during the ceremony... but there's a much better time."

"Yes?"

"Yes. In that fraction of a second before the final consummation. Although, of course, almost any time today would still be poetically satisfying."

Brooke said softly: "You love me very much, don't you, Kurtzie?"

In the third bed, Winton moved his bandaged wrists, moaned and cursed. "Shut up," he said. "Shut up. We've got to die—we know that. But why keep talking about it? Why talk?"

"Winton," said Kurtz, "doesn't like talk. Oh, no. He prefers action—only he bungles his actions. When you managed to steal that scalpel, Winton, why didn't you just cut your throat and have done with it? Didn't you realise the nurses would be bound to discover your cut wrists before anything serious happened? Or did you just go through the motions, with some half-witted idea of gaining sympathy?"

"I should have used it on you," said Winton. "It would have stopped your infernal talking."

"Minds," said Brooke. "Funny things. Look at yours, Kurtz. A good brain, education and experience behind it, a capacity to think constructively when you choose. Only, you don't choose. You prefer to twist and distort into the meanest, most personal, ugliest channels you can conceive. A real mental prostitution. And then there's you, Winton—no real mind at all, only a few cockeyed emotions. No intelligence. Just a sort of blind stretching forward to satisfy the need of the moment."

Winton said: "What do you know about what goes on in my mind? What about the scalpel? Could you have got one, Mr Genius?"

"If I wanted one," said Brooke, "I'd get one. And if I wanted to use it, I'd use it properly. I don't know how you got it, Winton, but I'm pretty certain it was by accident. And I'm not running down your lack of mind through malice. Oh no. You're the luckiest of the three of us. When you go, you've got so very little to lose."

Winton cursed. He repeated: "How do you know what I think about?"

"I don't—except by inference. But let's find out. Take this boiled egg, for instance. Here, let me hold it in my hand. Now, look at it, and tell me what you think."

As Winton hesitated, Kurtz laughed from his bed. "Come on, Winton, I want to hear this, too."

"It's just . . . an egg," said Winton. "Laid by a hen, on a farm somewhere. And boiled here in the kitchen."

"And brought to me, warm and white and unbroken," said Brooke. "I know. That's how your mind works. But this egg tells my mind a lot more."

"Like what?"

"Oh, many things . . . It reminds me, for instance, of Isaac Newton, of his discoveries—the law of gravitation—and from there, of space and time and the universe, of Einstein and relativity. And it reminds me on the other side, of pre-Newtonian science, of the theories of transmutation of metals;

and I see that Newton is the link, and the two sides of the chain meet again today in the atom physicists."

"You're talking nonsense," said Winton. "What has an egg to do with Isaac Newton?"

"Ah, so you haven't even heard *that* story? Let me tell it to you—maybe it will provide some consolation for you. It shows how even great minds have their moments of aberration... You see, a friend once came into Newton's kitchen, and there was the savant holding an egg in the palm of his hand—like this— staring at it in utter concentration—and on the stove next to him his watch boiled merrily in a pot of water."

Again, Kurtz laughed. Winton looked at Brooke uncertainly. He said: "You're still talking in the air..."

But Brooke was warming to his theme. "The human mind," he said, "what a magnificent mechanism! Properly applied, it creates miracles. Nothing, basically, is impossible—"

"Except us." In his triumph Winton spat. "What about us? All the best brains in science, all working on us, and they can't help. None of them can help."

Kurtz said: "All the same, Brooke's right. One day they'll find a cure. Maybe the day after you die, Winton. Or the day before. That's why your scalpel idea was so completely and utterly foolish."

"They still need data," said Brooke. "Sorry, I should have been more explicit. I should have said nothing is basically impossible when all the facts are known. Do you ever read detective stories?"

Winton said: "Trash."

"Not all of them. I'm thinking of a particular story, written by a man who's now dead—Jacques Futrelle. A magnificent story called *The Problem of Cell 13.* Futrelle's hero is a man he calls The Thinking Machine. He claimed that if he were locked in the condemned cell under the usual conditions, with nothing except his own magnificent mental equipment, he would *think* himself out. And he did, Winton, he did."

"In a story, yes. Anything's possible in a story."

"Logic is the common denominator between good fiction and

life. That's why I say your scalpel idea was clumsy. There are so many easier, more ingenious methods. Now, if I wanted to get rid of myself—"

"No," said Kurtz. "I don't like suicide—not even used as an example. Rather, assume that you were planning to kill Winton. Or better still, that I wanted to kill you. Much truer to life."

"All right, we'll say you want to kill me. And that you use your mind in the way you ought to use it. You'll pick something commonplace and apparently innocent, like—like this egg here. Yes, the egg's a good idea. First, you lay your hands on some virulent poison—if Winton could find a scalpel, you most certainly could find some poison. And you would work out a method of getting the poison inside the unbroken shell of the egg . . ."

Winton said: "That's an impossibility, Brooke, a complete impossibility."

"It it? That's what they said about The Thinking Machine and his guarded cell. And there's another angle, too—also from detective fiction. In a book called *The Three Coffins* one of the modern masters of detective fiction, John Dickson Carr, had his chief character giving a lecture on how to commit murder in a hermetically sealed room. If I remember correctly, there were three main methods, each with dozens of variations. And all perfectly possible—remember that, Winton. And if a murderer can get into a sealed room, commit a murder and disappear, he could also get into a sealed egg. The same principles apply. And the egg could be brought to me, like this one, through the normal innocent channels, and I could crack the shell, as I'm doing now, scoop up the egg—yes, do all the natural things, absolutely unsuspecting, put the spoon in my mouth, and die."

He put the spoonful of egg into his mouth.

And died.

"Mr le Roux," said Nurse Metter, and then: "No, I can't call you that. Hal has told me so much about you. I'm going to call you Rolf, and you must call me Doris. I can't go on calling my husband's best friend by his surname, can I?"

"Definitely not." The brown eyes twinkled, and behind the beard the full lips curved in a smile. "I would have liked to have come earlier, but Hal's letter didn't give me much time. Still, I suppose I'll have a chance for a chat with him before the ceremony?"

"Of course. The padre won't get here until after lunch, and you can see Hal as soon as he's finished his breakfast. He's in Ward 3, just down the passage. You can follow me in when I go to fetch the trays. They'll be ringing for me any second now."

Rolf thought of the letter from Hal in his pocket. And he thought: "Nice girl. If only Hal could live his normal span . . ."

The girl must have seen something of his mental images. "I'm afraid I'm just a little bit nervous," she said. "You see, it's not every day . . ."

She turned as the buzzer behind her sounded, and Rolf noticed that the numeral 3 had dropped in the indicator. But the buzzer kept on, urgently, insistently.

"Oh," said Doris Metter. "Something's wrong!"

She whirled past Rolf, moved in long-limbed strides down the passage. He came after her. Just inside the door of Ward 3 she paused momentarily, clutching her throat with one hand.

The contorted body of Hal Brooke sprawled in a half-sitting position on the bed, knees drawn up and twisted as though from a violent spasm. There was a thin line of froth on his lips.

Doris Metter said "Oh" again; she ran forward, stumbled over the tray and crockery on the floor, struggled back to her feet, and threw herself sobbing on the breast of the corpse on the bed.

Rolf le Roux said to the man in the bed opposite: "Keep ringing the bell." He put his hands on Doris Metter's shoulders, and gently drew her away. While doing so, he caught the elusive smell, bent over the body to make more certain. When he straightened again, his face was very grave.

Another nurse came to the door of the ward, hesitated only long enough to call out down the passage, and hurried forward. She caught the sobbing figure of Doris Metter in her arms and started to lead her gently from the room. They were only halfway to the door when the young doctor came in, took in the significance of the scene, and went to the living before the dead. He spoke quickly, consolingly; gave crisp instructions to the other nurses. Only then he came to look at the body.

He said to Rolf: "You're Mr le Roux, of course. Hal told me all about you. I'm Randall." And then: "This must have been a bad shock for you. Tragic, under the circumstances. But you must remember it could be expected to happen at any time."

Rolf's eyes were hard and implacable. "Smell his lips," he said.

Randall looked at him for a long second, then bent over the body. His expression also changed. He said: "I see."

The man in the bed opposite shook his head, as though to clear it. "Poison," he said conversationally. "And it was suicide, you know, even though it probably doesn't look like it. Brooke was talking about suicide just before it happened."

The third patient sat up in bed, waved a bandaged wrist. "You're a liar, Kurtz. He was talking about you killing him."

"Here," said Randall, suspiciously, "what's all this?"

"I'll tell you," said Kurtz. "I think I remember almost every word of the conversation. And don't interrupt until I've finished, Winton. You can say all you want to, then." Rapidly he sketched out the conversation. "Is that right?"

"That's right," said Winton grudgingly.

Dr Randall grimly got down on hands and knees, sniffed over the shattered egg that was lying on the floor, looked up, and nodded.

"And the egg," said Rolf, "was opened by Brooke? Is that all that happened?"

"That's all," said Winton.

Randall started to say: "There's no way of getting potassium cyanide into an unbroken—" He stopped, because Kurtz was shaking with laughter.

"Poor old Winton and his literal mind," said Kurtz. "How Brooke would have loved to hear him now! Of course something else happened, but something so casual and commonplace that Winton would never think of mentioning it."

"And that was?"

"Brooke cracked the egg, and took the spoonful to his mouth, and he was talking all the time. But between these two actions he did something else. He took the salt-cellar from the cruet, poured a quantity on the surface of the egg, and mixed it in with the spoon. And only then did he take his mouthful."

"You mean," asked Randall, "the salt . . .?" But while he was still speaking, Rolf was already on the floor, searching among the debris of the fallen tray.

"There it is," said Winton, "still lying on the bed."

Randall picked it up off the counterpane, unscrewed the top, and held the body of the container to his nose. He took one of the white grains, smelled it again to make sure, and touched it with his tongue. "No," he said, "this is ordinary table salt."

"So," said Kurtz, and looked quizzically at Rolf le Roux.

But Rolf said, almost to himself, "The timing . . ." and then, "How long did it take? I mean everything—from the moment the nurse left the breakfast trays to the moment she came back in answer to your ring?"

"Four or five minutes," said Kurtz.

"No," said Winton. "Longer than that. Say eight or nine."

"And all the time you both stayed in bed? You did not move?"

"I stayed in bed," said Winton. "But I don't know about Kurtz. I was too busy looking at Brooke to notice what Kurtz did."

Kurtz smiled. "I stayed in bed, too." He looked at Rolf. "You know, Brooke was a real admirer of yours. He advertised you—the great Sherlock of the Cape Town C.I.D. It's rather interesting to watch you now—standing there, baffled over Newton's egg."

"Not Newton's egg," said Rolf. "Newton's apple."

Except for the corpse, he was alone in the Ward. Kurtz and Winton had been searched and taken out. Dr Randall had gone down the passage to telephone the police post at Bossiesfontein.

He pulled the letter out of his pocket and read it again.

Dear Rolf,

If you ask me how I am, I will tell you that I am dying very nicely, thank you. Which is in direct contrast to the two other unfortunates in this ward. We all three are under sentence of death with intestinal T.B.; but, speaking strictly for myself, once you get accustomed to the feeling of general malaise and the knowledge that any given morning—if you will forgive the Irishism—you may wake up to find yourself dead, you can find some compensations, even in the valley of the shadow.

In my own case, I am delighted to find that my wits have never been so sharp and crystal-clear and—now hold on to your malodorous pipe!—I am also getting married.

Don't get a shock—it's all perfectly feasible and natural. I've checked with the quacks here, and read up all the authorities myself just to make sure, and this is certain—the disease, in the form I have it, is neither contagious nor infectious nor transmissible by heredity. Only fatal. And think of this, Rolf—I can still partially cheat death if I have a child.

And I'm *going* to have that child. It's all arranged. One of the doctors here by the name of Randall pulled strings—particularly decent of him because I think he's got a soft spot for Doris himself. (Oh, yes, of course, I should have told you—the girl is a nurse here, Doris Metter.) Anyway, he's doing everything possible. After the ceremony, we move straight into a private ward. Doris has been examined, too, and is 100 per cent healthy.

I know this all sounds like cold-blooded stud arrangements, but I may not have the time to waste on tact and social graces. I want a child, and I want a healthy child—one that has a chance to make better use of its life than I have.

Doris not only understands, she shares my urge. Last night she told me why. You see, she had an elder brother she worshipped, and he also died of an incurable disease—haemophilia—at the age of fourteen. I suppose there is basically some sort of Freudian identification in her mind between me and her brother, and she feels that in our child—and it'll be a son for sure—she'll have me and her brother too. But that's not entirely the whole story for either of us. You see, oldtimer, we're really in love.

The ceremony is on Tuesday—and don't you dare send me your congratulations by letter. I want to hear them verbally, direct from the labyrinths of your beard. If you catch a train from Cape Town on Sunday night, you should be here on the morning of the marriage, the lucky day.

More when I see you in the flesh—

Hal.

Not the letter of a suicide, thought Rolf. And yet, in three days much could happen. The half-life he was living, the twisted motives . . .

To decide definitely, there were many other things to be found out. Access to poisons, for instance. Opportunity, generally. More facts were needed, new angles. Sometimes, looked at from a different direction, the impossible became obvious . . . and he owed it to Hal to make absolutely sure.

Rolf found Dr Randall sitting at the desk in the office along the passage. He asked: "Have you contacted the police?"

"No," said Randall. "I was . . . well, to tell the truth, I was waiting for you. I wanted to have a talk."

"Yes?"

"I. . . Look here, *must* I call the police? Won't you forget about the poison—let me sign a death certificate? What good will it do with the police prying around, badgering Dor—Nurse Metter? What for? Isn't it enough that Hal's dead, without him also being branded a suicide? Isn't it really better my way?"

Rolf said: "Maybe it would be . . . easier. But what if it was not suicide? Would you want his murderer to go scot-free?"

Randall was deeply upset. "Don't forget, he was a doomed man in any case. And who could have killed him? Kurtz? Winton? Also doomed men. Is it worthwhile putting all this further torture on a innocent girl?"

"Hal Brooke was my friend," said Rolf. He sat for a moment,

with his eyes far away. "For his sake, and if I were *sure* . . . but I first have to be sure, you understand. We can wait two hours, and after that I promise you I will make up my mind."

"Thank you, Mr le Roux. And if I can help in any way . . . ?"

"First, I'd like to know where the poison could have come from."

"In all probability from this room. From that closet over there."

"Locked?"

"Well, yes—but actually the lock slips if you give a sharp jerk on the door. We should have had it repaired, of course, only . . . well, it's just been neglected."

Rolf was staring at the serried bottles and jars on the shelf. He located the tiny potassium cyanide container, and scratched his beard contemplatively. He said: "One thing I don't understand . . . there are poisons here, yes, but there are also harmless drugs. Isn't it unusual to keep them together?"

"Not if you realise that, being so far from town, we dispense most of our own medicines, and that this room is our dispensary."

"Even so, isn't potassium cyanide rather a strange drug to have here?"

"No. It's a common drug in a T.B. hospital. It's used in making up a very effective cough mixture. A tiny quantity, of course—the basis is a minim two drops to eight ounces of other ingredients."

"I see. And so it is perfectly possible for one of the patients to walk in here, if he knows about the room, jerk open the locked cupboard, and remove a quantity of poison? Could it be done unseen?"

"Definitely. It was from this room, we think, that Winton stole the scalpel with which he tried to commit suicide. But it would have to be done late at night. During the day, if I'm not here, there's a nurse on duty."

"Have you actually noticed that anything here was interfered with at any time?"

"No. I can honestly say I've *seen* nothing . . ."

"But?"

"Well, when I came and sat down here just now, I had a feeling that there was something wrong, something out of place. Just a *vague* feeling . . ."

She lay on the bed in the darkened room, and if she had been weeping the atmosphere of tragedy would have seemed less.

"There's nothing to talk about," she said. "It's just . . . horrible. And I don't think you would understand."

"Perhaps I would," said Rolf. "He was my friend, you know. And he wrote me all about the situation. Let *me* talk, rather. You can tell me whether I am right . . . You see, I know what he wanted—how he felt about having a child. And how you felt. And it seems to me that, even though you loved him, the horror is not so much Hal dying. You knew it would happen, and you were prepared for it. No, the horror in your mind is that the child will never be born, that Hal will not live again in your child, that you have nothing of him left . . ."

She started to cry—hoarse, racking sobs. "Yes," she said, "yes." And then: "I couldn't even give him his last wish." She heaved convulsively in her sobbing. "I had a brother once—" and then gave herself over to a paroxysm of grief. After a while she quieted. "He wanted a child so badly. That's the irony of it. So badly that . . . and his face, when he heard from Dr Randall that I had been examined, that there was nothing wrong with me, that I could have his son, a healthy son . . . That was all he had left in life, Rolf."

He waited for her, then he asked: "When you brought him his tray in the morning, was there anything about it that was *different*?"

"No," she said. "It was his usual breakfast. A soft-boiled egg and coffee."

"And the others in the ward—did they also have boiled eggs?"

"No. Kurtz's egg was fried, and Winton had an omelette."

"Was Hal's egg in any way cracked?"

"No. It was just an egg. I gave the order in the kitchen, and a few minutes later took the three trays in."

"And after that?"

"I had more trays to carry to other wards. And then I heard that you were here, and I came to speak to you. You know . . . the rest."

"Yes. But tell me this—from the time you took Hal his tray to the moment we went back to the ward, how long do you think it was?"

"A long time," she said. "At least twenty-five minutes."

Rolf le Roux came back to the dispensary, sat down at the desk, and put his head in his hands. Motive, he thought, that was the key . . . the motive for suicide—or murder. And he thought again of that last conversation in the ward, the dying man's lecture on Jacques Futrelle and John Dickson Carr. A sealed egg, yes, and Isaac Newton . . . looking at the egg while the watch boiled . . . the law of gravitation . . .

Because his thoughts were travelling in circles he opened his eyes, emptied his mind, and looked around the room.

And looking, he felt what the doctor had experienced before him, the vague unease that a pattern was wrong, that something was out of position. And right in front of his eyes, on the bookshelf above the desk he saw what it was.

The huge volumes of the *British Encylopaedia of Medical Practice* Volumes 1, 2, 3, 4, 5, 7, 6, 8—volumes 7,6. One out of place. Which?

The index of volume 7 told him nothing. He turned to volume 6. Gout, granuloma, guinea-worm disease, haemetemesis, haematoporphyrinuria, haematuria, haemophilia, haem—haemophilia. He remembered Hal's letter.

Page 123. Definition: An hereditary disease, only affecting males. Prognosis: grave. A fatal illness, and generally fatal in childhood. Females cannot have it, but they do transmit it to male offspring. *And Doris's brother had died of haemophilia.* That meant the disease had been transmitted through her mother. And if Doris herself had a *male* child it would . . . No, that wasn't quite right. Her male child *might* have haemophilia. Not would.

I know something about genetics, thought Rolf, and yet I very nearly made that mistake. A layman reading the first paragraphs and then skipping over the formulae beneath would almost certainly fall into the mental trap, be *sure* that if Doris bore a boy it would certainly be a haemophiliac.

Here was a motive. Yes, for suicide. If Hal, with his searching curiosity had crept in here last night, had looked at the book—how would he have reacted? The poison closet so handy . . . but where would he keep it? What would he use as a container? Would he, with his tidy mind, have destroyed himself without warning Doris of the peril of her blood?

And besides, it was a motive for murder too. Randall, in love with Doris, fond of Hal . . . Suppose he only heard last night that her brother had died of the disease. Suppose he came here to check the truth, and he knew about Hal's urge for the child, and Doris's . . . Might he not have resolved to kill to save her future misery? He had been anxious enough to sign a death certificate . . . No. Not a doctor. Such reasoning would be incredible for a doctor.

Could it be something else, something apart from this, some motive pointing the finger at Kurtz or Winton?

The truth . . .

He saw it. And the room whirled.

Isaac Newton, he thought. How it all came back to him. The talk about the egg . . . and then the proof that Kurtz had actually named the murder weapon. The saltcellar. Because if a man took salt from a cruet stand, when finished he would most likely replace the cellar in the cruet. Especially if he were eating off the limited surfaces of a tray. Or he would put it on the tray. And in his death paroxysms, if the cruet, the tray, everything fell to the floor, then the saltcellar would also fall. Like Newton's apple, obeying the law of gravitation. And if the saltcellar were found on the bed, then someone must have put it there. Or rather, put an *innocent* saltcellar on the bed—

After gaining possession of the poisoned one.

And then there was the final irrefutable psychological proof: the perception of time.

Newton and his egg again. A subtlety—the great man's mind was wandering into absent-minded reverie, because although he was staring at what he thought was his watch, he wasn't really seeing it. His mind was wandering because he knew that if he concentrated on his watch *the egg would seem to take longer to boil.*

Kurtz said four or five minutes; Winton said eight or nine. But Doris Metter thought it was twenty-five minutes. *Because she had been waiting for it to happen.*

And Rolf saw her again, in the cold light of his mind, stumble over the tray on the floor, rise to her feet, weep on the breast of the corpse. And the actions formed two clear patterns. Picking up the poisoned saltcellar, putting down the innocent one.

But he saw also another image. He saw her, last night, the night before her wedding day, standing in the dispensary, picking up the medical book on a curious impulse, reading, and having her whole world collapse in a few lines. And he saw into her mind, too, into the torment and chaos, crystallising in the soul-tearing illogic of her resolution. In his ears again he heard her voice, bubbling through her tears: "I couldn't even give him his last wish, Rolf—not even his last wish."

Rolf le Roux stood up, slowly and heavily, and he walked along the corridor until he met Dr Randall, and he said: "I have made a mistake. You may sign the death certificate."

THE BIG FIX

Herbert Harris

"YOU LOOK HOT," the barmaid said. "Just ready for a cool drink."

"I feel hot, too," Jake told her. "It's warm work humping those apple-barrels in the market."

He wished he could stop sweating. Nerves, of course—not the apple-barrels.

The girl behind the bar looked like June. He felt a stab of remorse. He hadn't really wanted to kill her, though some might say the little bitch had asked for it.

In her strange way, she'd been fond of him. She'd even tried to help him. But that hadn't made up for her outward contempt, the humiliation.

Hardly more than half a glass of beer had passed his lips when the two men closed in on him. A pincer movement, one on each side, quietly and efficiently.

Both men seemed huge. Just one of them would have been enough. After all, Jake was only small, slightly built, nervous-looking, incapable—one would say—of violence.

"Your name Jake Culley?" The larger of them put the question.

"It is."

"What's that in your jacket pocket? Mind if we see?"

Jake shrugged, smiled bleakly. "Okay, the game's up, isn't it? Some kind friend grassed on me, eh? How much did you pay the lousy little snout for his tip-off?"

"Never mind that," one of the detectives said.

Jake pulled the packets from his pocket. A bundle of white paper packets, each with its dose of deadly ecstasy, fastened together with a rubber band. He handed them to the C.I.D.

man, who opened one, looked at the contents, screwed his face up with disgust.

"Quite a few 'fixes' in this lot. What do you charge the junkies for them? Two nicker a kick? . . . three? . . . five?"

Jake stared back in sullen silence.

"Who pays you for running them around? Who's the pusher?"

"I never knew who the pusher was," Jake said. "A geezer acts as go-between and gives me my commission. I don't know this one's name either."

"Or maybe you're just suffering from loss of memory," the detective said acidly. "How much more of this dope have you got at home?"

Jake tightened his lips sulkily.

"Let's go back to your pad and have a look, shall we?" the C.I.D. man suggested. He wrapped a big hand tightly round Jake's arm. "Come on."

Jake and the two detectives got into the police-car. One of them asked, "Where to?" and Jake told them with reluctant hesitation. The car moved off, nosing its way to where his wife lay murdered.

"You got any kids?" one of the policemen asked.

"No."

"Thought not. If you had, you wouldn't be peddling this filthy dope to the teenagers. Are you married?"

"Yes."

Not strictly true any more, he thought. *Was* married. Now a widower. A very, very short time a widower. June's body would scarcely have had time to grow cold.

Maybe the remorse he felt sprang from his dislike of violence. It wasn't that he minded her being dead. She had preferred Tony Brunner for a long time now.

Looking back, Jake realised he should have known better than to marry her. If he hadn't been such a simpleton, it probably would never have happened.

She had been as anxious as hell to get out of that club where she worked as a hostess. He hadn't realised what a hostess was. When you came to London from a small provincial backwater, there was a hell of a lot you had to learn.

"I'm joining a Group," he had told her excitedly. "As a guitarist. Reckon I'll be really in the money in about six months."

She had believed him. It was the prospect of money that had attracted her. Not so much his naïve boyish appeal as the dough he looked like making.

He had no illusions about himself. As a lover he had always been as hammy as anyone could be. That didn't matter such a lot to June. She could have all the affairs on the side that she wanted.

It was sheer bad luck when the Group flopped. Even worse luck to find that guitarists were ten a penny, and guitarists a lot better than himself were looking for other ways to scratch a living.

So Jake had got the job with a wholesaler in the fruit and vegetable market. The fact that his old man had been a greengrocer had helped. Not much money, but enough to pay the rent on their crummy flat and buy a few necessaries at the supermarket.

He had known June wouldn't be satisfied, and she wasn't.

"I've got a part-time job," she had said, sullen and aggressive. He was no longer in any doubt that she not only didn't love him any more—if she ever did—but that she even felt sorry for him.

"Where?"

"At Tony Brunner's Discotheque—helping out."

"You know what they say about Brunner? He'll make a pass at anything in a skirt."

His wife's dark eyes smouldered. "Why the hell should I care what they say? If you want to keep me prisoner in this rotten hole of a flat, then you'd better go and earn a bit more money. If not, then let me earn a bit extra in whatever way I like."

"I'll make the grade one of these days," Jake said. "Then it'll be all right, love, won't it? I mean, if I could raise the capital I could open my own shop . . ."

"Where would you raise the capital?"

He smiled wearily. "Maybe your new boss would lend it. He's got plenty, I believe." His face darkened. "Not that I'd want you to sell yourself or anything. By God, if I thought he was making a pass at you, I'd carve him up."

"You?" She laughed at him derisively. "You couldn't carve up a pound of liver!"

It stung like hell, but he knew she was right. He would never stand a chance in a brush with Tony Brunner.

"Big" Brunner they sometimes called him. A large heavily-built man, quick-tempered. He had a lot of friends, too, fellows you wouldn't care to turn your back on at night in a dark alley.

And, of course, Brunner had money. You could see that by his snazzy car and swish clothes.

How would June earn the money Brunner gave her? What would he expect from her? Maybe it wasn't important any more if she had an affair with him. And yet the thought of Brunner mauling her about made him break out in a prickly sweat.

One day she had said to him: "Do you really want to make some lolly?—some lolly worth having, I mean?"

Jake looked blankly at her. "Why?"

"Tony feels sorry for you, as I do. He thinks you've had a raw deal. He says if you really want to get a bit of capital behind you, he might help."

"Conscience, is it?"

"How do you mean?"

"A reward for allowing him to mess about with my wife? I saw what happened in his car when he brought you home."

June's face flushed a deep red. Her eyes blazed. "Look," she said angrily, "Tony's a good bloke. He's doing you a favour. Do you want to go on living in this stinking hole?"

Jake swallowed. He supposed, deep down, he was still in love with her. He was prepared to believe that she might—just *might*—have his interests sincerely at heart.

"What's he want me to do?" he asked.

"You'd better talk to Tony himself about that."

Jake had gone to talk to Brunner. Like a good little boy. Weak as water. Pushed around as usual. And that's how he came to be selling "fixes" to the local junkies, putting more money into the pocket of a prosperous pusher named Brunner.

Flogging the heroin and coke meant six times the dough the fruit wholesaler was paying him. That needed a lot of resisting.

Maybe, he thought, if he made a pile quickly and could find a ritzier place and pamper June a bit, she might start respecting him again, might even get to loving him. . . .

"You're so kind, so gentle," she had said once.

Big Brunner could never be that. Brunner was too crude and violent. She'd find out, sooner or later, which of the two was better to live with.

Then came the moment he would never forget, when the taste of disillusionment was at its bitterest.

"You were quite right about Tony and me necking in the car," she said, a dreamy wistful expression on her face, as if she were revelling in telling him. "We've done it several times. I love him. Do you understand?"

"No, you couldn't love him," Jake said. "Not *him* . . ."

"I'm leaving you, Jake. I'm going away with Tony. It's all arranged. I'm sorry, but I've made up my mind."

"But you can't want to go and live with that cheap lousy crook! It doesn't make sense!"

"Look," June said, "I'll not have you calling Tony names. If anyone deserves to be called names, it's you. You're a weak-kneed, namby-pamby failure. You'll never be anything but a flop as long as you live. You aren't fit to clean Tony Brunner's shoes!"

He had always tried to be peaceable. He'd never let his temper get on top of him before. But now he knew he couldn't do anything about the great seething bubble of rage that rose up inside him.

"You hate me, don't you?" he snarled through clenched teeth.

"Yes!" she shouted at him. *"Yes!"*

"And I hate you, too, you bitch!"

Without knowing what he was doing, he threw himself at her. He seized her throat and squeezed and squeezed, and then the terrible sounds stopped coming out of her and she lay on her back on the bed staring lifelessly at the ceiling.

He turned away from her, sweating, half sobbing. And he looked at the note on her dressing-table. *I'll call for you at twelve, T.*

So she was going away with him at noon. Lover Boy would be picking her up, and they'd be off to some sun-kissed spot to live it up on Brunner's money.

He caught hold of a fistful of June's dress and tore it open all the way down the front. Then he took some of the packets of dope from a drawer and stuffed them in his pocket.

Once away from the flat, he found a public call-box.

"Hello . . . police?" Jake said. "You won't know me. I'm just tipping you off about something. I hate these filthy scum who live on junkies. You'll find a bloke with dope on him in the Three Bells . . . Bridge Street . . . name of Jake Culley. This isn't a hoax, but genuine. So long, copper."

When he rang off he walked to the Three Bells in Bridge Street. God, he felt hot. He could do with a long cool beer.

The police turned up and arrested him just as he had wanted them to. And they had suggested going back to his flat to look for more dope—or some information about the pusher—just as he had wanted them to.

And as they went there in the police-car, Jake said, "Look, my wife doesn't know about this racket, so don't get her mixed up in it, will you? She's a nice kid, and I'm fond of her, and I'm only flogging this stuff to make a bit more money and take her away from the stinking hole we're living in."

"Okay, chum, take it easy," one of the C.I.D. men said.

And, then, just as he had hoped, they got there dead on time, and Tony Brunner was there. The discotheque owner drug-pusher sat by the bed, his head in his hands, moaning.

"My God!" Jake screamed, rushing into the room. "What have you done to my wife? What have you done to June?"

He threw himself on the dead girl on the bed and kissed her, sobbing. There were real tears streaming from his eyes—he hadn't expected that he could cry real tears.

"Oh, my poor June . . . my darling . . . my poor *baby* . . ."

And then he was on his feet, and he hurled himself at Tony Brunner. "You lousy rotten murderer! You dirty filthy. . .!"

The two detectives tore him away from June's lover, and once again they were saying, "Okay, okay, take it easy now"—and they held him in a vice-like grip while he glared at Brunner.

So far, so good. He wasn't sure what he'd get for peddling drugs. Couple of years maybe? But Brunner would get ten or fifteen years. He'd been shoved around too long. So now he was shoving the others around, and that was fine.

THE WOMAN AFRAID OF OCTOBER

Julian Symons

Eve Addle, as her friend Mary Morthouse told Francis Quarles, was rather simple and very respectable. Those two facts were the clues to her sad story.

For most of her life Eve's story was not sad, but merely humdrum. Her parents were killed in an air crash when she was four years old, and Eve was brought up by her strict Presbyterian maiden Aunt Clarice. Eve was twelve years old and a normal, although timid child, easily distressed by the wit of the schoolgirls who called after her, "Poor old Eve, she's addled", when Aunt Clarice felt it a duty to make her revelation. The father and mother whom the girl only distantly remembered had not, Aunt Clarice said with a snap of her wide thin mouth, been married.

Eve's first reaction was simple bewilderment. "But why not?"

"Because your mother still had a husband alive."

"Couldn't they be—divorced?" Eve didn't know much about such things, but she had heard the word.

"Her husband was a Roman Catholic. He refused to divorce her." The corners of Aunt Clarice's thin mouth turned down, almost in a crescent. "Your mother and father lived together in sin."

The girl did not fully understand the implications of what she was being told, but she sensed the cold malice behind the words. "They didn't," she cried, and beat upon her aunt's hard corseted person with her firsts. "They didn't live in sin."

"They lived and died in sin," Aunt Clarice repeated. "And you were conceived in sin. I have felt it my duty to look after you, but I expect no good of an illegitimate child."

Within a few years Eve was free of Aunt Clarice, and working as a clerk in a London store, but from emotional shocks so cruelly delivered in childhood one is never really free. She grew up into a quiet nervous woman, respectable and shy, who told nobody of her deeply shameful secret. She was in general the least malicious of women, but when the question of illegitimacy was mentioned, Eve Addle spoke with a venom almost worthy of Aunt Clarice of the sluts who allowed men to have their way with them before marriage. For the most part, however, Eve was not consciously discontented with her humdrum life. She ruled her actions, other than those which involved going to and from the office, by a daily casting of her horoscope, supplemented by the advice of Dr Mayland Rayther, given in her favourite magazine, *The Stars Foretell.* It was not until a distant relative died and left her five thousand pounds and a house called Hammersley Hall, that Eve Addle thought about changing her name.

Her benefactor's name was Ezra Lammas, and he had lived most of his life in Canada. He was the brother-in-law of some long-dead uncle, and although Eve did not remember him at all he had a vivid recollection of dandling her on his knee when she was eighteen months old and he was paying a visit to what he insisted on calling the Old Country. Ezra Lammas had always meant to come back to live in the Old Country, and it was with this intention that he had bought Hammersley Hall.

The house was situated just outside Byfield, in one of the least accessible parts of Essex, and Eve went down and looked at it one day. Hammersley Hall was a large decaying Georgian house with Victorian additions, a house which might have been used to illustrate a thesis that not all old houses are worth preserving. Nevertheless, Eve was enchanted. She went to see the Byfield estate agent, Mr Baker.

"Yes," Mr Baker said. "The house has been on our books for some time, at quite a low rental. The last tenant moved out about two years ago. He complained of damp. Not a very saleable property, I fear."

"I don't want to sell it. I want to live in it."

"*Live* in it," Mr Baker said. He recovered himself rapidly. "Of course, Mrs Addle. Do you have a large family?"

"*Miss* Addle," Eve said. It was then that she began to think about changing her name.

Her method of doing so may be thought foolish, but it is not so very unusual for rather timid spinsters. She bought a paper called *Sweet Matrimony* and answered three of the advertisements in it. She described herself as in her early thirties (she was thirty-nine), and her hair as blonde (it was darkish mouse). Otherwise her letters were strictly truthful. She asked for the exact birth dates of the advertisers.

She received two replies. One she ruled out immediately. He had been born under Libra, a sign always unlucky to her. The other letter was from a widower named John Smith, whose dear wife had passed on. He was a home-lover, fond of animals (she interpreted this to include her parrot Timothy), had been wounded in the war, was not rich but had some independent means, and wanted to settle down again. He gave his age as forty-three and enclosed a snapshot, which showed a sturdy dependable-looking pipe-smoking figure.

Eve liked the photograph, but what really decided her was the fact that John Smith, like herself, had been born under Capricorn. She cast their horoscopes carefully, and everything seemed to augur well. Within a week they had met, within a month they were married. They spent a few days at Bournemouth, and early in October moved into Hammersley Hall.

This was the story—with the exception of the shameful secret, which of course she didn't know—that Eve's friend Mary Morthouse told to Francis Quarles. Miss Morthouse was a thin fluttery birdlike woman, and there could be no doubt that she was troubled.

"You see, Mr Quarles, he never really wanted to meet me, Mr Smith I mean, don't you think that was strange when Eve and I are such friends, lived in the same house, her flat's just below mine, and we cast our horoscopes together?"

"Did you meet him?"

"Just once, for ten minutes, when he came to call for her. He seemed quite a gentleman," she admitted reluctantly. "But then there was the strange way they got married, just going off without telling anybody. I happen to know that some of her friends at Taylor's, that's the store where she worked, were rather upset. And then you'd think they'd have asked me down to see them, wouldn't you? It seems unnatural that they shouldn't."

Privately, Quarles thought that it was not at all unnatural, but he said patiently, "I don't quite see what you want me to do."

"Something's wrong, I can feel it. Just look at these letters that Eve's sent me since they've been married."

There were three letters and a postcard, written in a spidery but elegant hand. The postcard was the first in order of date. It was sent from Bournemouth, and simply said that they were having a wonderful time. The letters were all from Hammersley Hall. The first thanked Mary for the beautiful silver teapot and milk jug, which they would always treasure, and said that John had wanted a quiet wedding and that she knew Mary would understand that they hadn't asked a soul, and had even got the witnesses from the street. The second, written evidently in reply to a suggestion from Miss Morthouse that she should pay a visit, said evasively that there were a great many things to get straight, but that she and John hoped to see her dear Mary very soon. The last letter, written four days ago and evidently set down in haste, was of quite a different kind.

Dear Mary,

I am dreadfully afraid that I have made a mistake. You will remember that three years ago I had my accident under Libra, and that Edgar died under Libra too. I am convinced that we made a terrible mistake in moving here under Libra. I have made a discovery, and it means nothing but bad luck, most terribly bad luck, and I don't know what to do about it. I have consulted Doctor Rayther, but he has been no help. I can't see any way out. I wish I knew what to do. Timothy sends his love.

Eve

"As soon as I got this letter, I knew that Eve needed me."

"Just a moment. Who is Doctor Rayther?"

"Oh, that's Doctor Mayland Rayther, who writes in *The Stars*

Foretell. Eve and I guide our actions by what he advises. If he was unable to help, things must be serious. And you see that she doesn't even mention Mr Smith in this letter."

"I noticed that. Go on."

"I went down to Hammersley Hall. It's a cold dank place, I wouldn't live there if you paid me, and I don't know how Eve does. But I do know that she was frightened, Mr Quarles."

"What of?"

"What could she be afraid of but *him*? Of course," she added, with one of those lapses into astrological terminology that Quarles was beginning to recognise, "she was always afraid of Libra and Scorpio. I mean, of October."

"Of October?"

"Libra and Scorpio are her unlucky signs, and they both come in October, partly at least. October is her unlucky month."

"Who was Edgar?"

"He was her cat, and he died in October. Then the accident she mentions, when she was knocked down and broke a rib, that was in October too."

"What about this discovery that she mentions in the letter. Did you ask about that?"

"Yes. But all she would say was that it meant bad luck for her. Then she started to say something about her father and mother, and stopped."

They did not seem to be getting far. "She didn't say that she was afraid of her husband?"

"No. But his manner towards her had quite changed, he was bullying, unpleasant. He seemed to hate Timothy."

"Timothy?"

"That's her parrot. He talks, you know, and began to imitate Mr Smith. Really, it was quite comical, but he didn't think so. 'If you don't shut that bird up, I will,' he said to her, although he didn't just say bird. He swore." Quarles nodded sympathetically. "So then she threw a rug over Timothy's cage, and he stopped. Then later on he shouted at her, really *shouted* at her, because the scones she had made for tea were a little burned. And I can tell you something else. He wanted to get me away from the house as soon as he could. At six o'clock he looked at his watch and said he would drive me to the station."

"Did you talk while he drove you?"

"He said that Eve was nervy. But it was more than that, it was as though—as though she were somewhere else." She leaned forward. "I believe he means to kill her, Mr Quarles."

Quarles was sceptical about this. He was inclined to believe that Miss Morthouse's fears were two-thirds fantasy and the other third astrological divination. But he called next day at the offices of *Sweet Matrimony.*

A well-preserved woman in her forties received him in the offices, which consisted of two rather shabby rooms on a third floor in Pimlico. The woman wore a tight black coat and skirt dotted with costume jewellery. Her voice was a melodious coo.

"Good morning. Do sit down." Quarles sat down. She drew out a form from a pile in front of her. "I am Jennifer Lamprey, and I edit *Sweet Matrimony*. Now, may I have your name please."

"Francis Quarles."

"Sex, well, I can see that." Her smile bent the perfect cupid's bow of her lipstick. "You are a British subject?"

"Yes."

"And unmarried, naturally."

"Well, as a matter of fact, no. I've got four wives living, divorced of course, but my fifth is still around. We shall be severing the nuptial ties in a couple of months, and then I shall be ready for number six." His smile was as sickly sweet as her own.

Mrs Lamprey registered first incredulity, then anger. "If this is a joke, I think it in very poor taste."

"You're perfectly right. I was overwhelmed by your technique, I apologise. I want some information." Quarles produced his card.

The coo disappeared. Her voice was as sharp as a saw. "What about?"

"First of all, can you tell me what happens when somebody puts an advertisement in *Sweet Matrimony*?"

"Yes, I can do that. All advertisements are keyed with box

numbers, and we ask that no names and addresses should be given in the first instance. We ask also that for the protection of our clients the first meeting should take place in this office. We take details of our clients' occupations, financial situation, and so on."

"What proof do you have that they are telling the truth?"

"Proof? The proof is in the number of happy marriages we have arranged." Her pen tapped the desk. "Come to the point, Mr Quarles."

"Very well. Do you remember arranging a meeting between a man named John Smith and a woman named Eve Addle?"

"It is against our policy to give information about our clients."

Quarles spread his large hands on the table. "A friend of Miss Addle—Mrs Smith, as she is now—has been in touch with me. She is convinced that Mr Smith intends some harm to his wife. Unless you can convince me that Mr Smith's background is above reproach, I shall go to the police."

"I didn't know they were married." Mrs Lamprey was badly shaken. "They're supposed to tell us. But, of course, I can't take any responsibility—"

"I'm not going to argue," Quarles said brutally. "You can show me what you've got, or I'll go to Scotland Yard."

Half an hour later he had gone through the slender files on John Smith and Eve Addle. Mr Smith had given an address in St John's Wood, where he said he had lived for several years, and had said that he was a retired woollen merchant of independent means.

"He seemed a nice steady sort of chap," Mrs Lamprey recalled. "Attractive in a fatherly kind of way. You know, smoked a pipe and looked at you very straight. He had rather fine eyes, a sort of steel blue, magnetic eyes you might call them. She was quite bowled over, I could see that. She's a very quiet little woman, mouselike I'd suppose you'd call her. I remember she asked him if he liked parrots, because she was devoted to her parrot Timothy, and he laughed and said there wasn't a bird or an animal he wasn't fond of. After that first introduction they're supposed to let us know if they want to—go on any further, as it were—but we can't compel them to do that."

"There's nothing else you can remember about the interview?"

"Not really." She hesitated. "There was just one thing, nothing to do with the interview really, but she was very embarrassed about it. Her mother and father weren't married, and this seemed to weigh on her mind. She told it to me in the strictest confidence—she thought of it as a terrible social stigma and regarded me as a sort of mother confessor—and asked whether I thought she should tell him. I told her not to be silly—it was something that concerned herself, and nobody else."

Quarles nodded, and went off to investigate Mr Smith's home in St John's Wood. He found that it was an accommodation address, a tobacconist's shop where letters were received. The man behind the counter remembered Mr Smith, a pleasant sort of gentleman who came in twice a week for his letters, and always had a cheerful word. "Last time I saw him he said he'd be away for a few weeks," the tobacconist said. "And since then there've been no letters."

An hour later a grim-faced Quarles took a tearful Mrs Lamprey along to Scotland Yard. There she looked through a book of photographs, and put her finger on one. The face she indicated was square, solid, dependable, the sort of face you connect with a good honest beer-drinking British citizen.

"Pedro Martinez," said the sergeant who stood at her shoulder. "Alias Charles Jones, John Smith, Edgar Brown, William Robinson, Robert Williams. Got a string of convictions as long as your arm, all for fraud and false pretences. Specialises in spinsters who want a man, goes through a marriage ceremony with them if necessary, persuades them that since they're sharing all their worldly goods they should have a joint bank account, draws out the cash and off he goes. Funny thing is, he really has got a wife who's fond of him. She drifts around the country and he goes back to her for a few weeks or months at a time after he's pulled a successful job."

"Has he any record of violence?"

"No violence. Conceited, like most of them, very proud of his triumphs, talks about them if he gets the chance. But violence, no. He just takes the money and skips. What's he been up to now?"

Quarles told him. Then they all went to see Superintendent Leeds. The Superintendent reduced Mrs Lamprey to tears with a few well-chosen words, and agreed that it might be a good thing if he accompanied Quarles down to Hammersley Hall.

It was raining, a thin persistent rain, as they drove through a pair of rusting iron gates, and up a weed-grown drive.

"I hope we're in time," Leeds said. "From what the friend —what was her name, Miss Morthouse?—said about Smith's bad temper, I should guess that she was holding out about agreement to the joint bank account."

"Probably," Quarles said. His thoughts seemed far away. "We can only hope that she's still holding out. If she's signed the agreement I'm afraid he'll have hopped it. Here we are. Pretty grim, isn't it?"

Hammersley Hall, ivy-covered and with every ivy leaf apparently dripping with rain, what could be seen of the façade stained and peeling, certainly did not look particularly prepossessing, yet Quarles could see the appeal its decayed romanticism might hold for somebody like Eve Addle. The slamming of their car door in the courtyard had a curious effect of finality. Quarles pulled the iron bell outside, and the sound clanged through the house. Nobody came to the door. He pulled at the bell again. Now the door was suddenly opened, and a little woman stood there. Her hands and knees were dirty, there was dirt in her untidy hair, her eyes were red. She looked at them.

"Mrs Smith?" Leeds asked gently. He gave her his card. "May we come in?"

Like somebody in a dream she led them through a dark empty hall, smelling of damp, and then into a drawing-room almost equally dark. There was no fire in the grate, but somebody had been burning paper. One or two yellow unburned fragments lay among the ash.

"I'm sorry," she said. "I'm afraid I—you see, it's the maid's day off."

"It's really your husband I want—"

"Hallo, hallo, hallo," a raucous voice cried. "How are you?"

"It's only Timothy," Mrs Smith said, with a look of pleasure that gave her face a faded prettiness. In one corner of the room there could be seen a malevolent-looking parrot of gaudy plumage. The Superintendent crossed over, said "Pretty Polly" and put out a hand. A moment later he yelped with pain and the parrot screeched with laughter.

"Pretty Polly," he repeated derisively, and then said sternly, "I'm Timothy the Terrible, Timothy the Terrible."

"Oh *dear*," she said. "He doesn't like being called Pretty Polly, it always makes him cross. I do hope he hasn't hurt your finger. Let me look."

While she was looking, Quarles bent down and extracted the yellowed papers from the grate. They were newspaper cuttings, and three or four of them were still perfectly readable.

"Mrs Smith," Leeds said, in a tone perceptibly sharpened by his encounter with the parrot, "the person we really want to see is your husband."

"I'm afraid you can't. He's gone. He left last night."

"Then it's too late. Did you sign an agreement saying that he could draw cheques on your joint account?"

"Why yes," she said. "Mr Smith is my husband. I thought it was only right."

From the corner came the parrot's voice. "I'm Mr Smith, I'm Mr Smith."

"Be quiet, Timothy. He's rather jealous, I'm afraid." Now she brightened. "My husband is away on business. He'll only be a couple of days. He has some property at Weston-super-Mare, and had to attend to some details about it. I don't understand business."

"That's what he told you? That he'd be back in a couple of days?"

"Of course. You can see him then."

"Mrs Smith," Quarles said, "what was the discovery you made—the one you told your friend Mrs Morthouse about in your letter?"

She passed a hand over her forehead. "I—just can't remember. Did I say that?"

"You said the discovery was bad luck, terribly bad luck, and you didn't know what to do about it."

"I don't remember."

"Was it these you'd discovered?" Quarles held out the fragments of newspaper cuttings to Leeds. "Like many men who make a profession of deceiving women, Smith enjoyed keeping a record of his successes. These are cuttings about a few of the women he'd 'married' and left. This was the discovery, wasn't it? That you weren't Mrs Smith, but still only Eve Addle."

She said nothing, looked down at her hands. The bird cried, "Silly old Addle."

"That meant something very important to you, didn't it? Much more, even, than it does to most people. Because your parents couldn't get married, and you'd always thought of it as something shameful. And so when you found that you had gone through a marriage ceremony but weren't married, that must have been particularly awful for you."

"It was cruel," she whispered. "Cruel."

"It was cruel, yes. But not a reason for murdering him. How did you do it? And why are your hands and knees so dirty? What have you just been doing?"

Now Leeds was on his feet, speaking indignantly. "Really, Quarles, I can't listen to this kind of thing. You haven't a shred of real evidence to back up these wild accusations. If Mrs Smith—Miss Addle—likes to bring an action for slander I shall be compelled—"

He was interrupted by a squawk from the corner. "You've poisoned me," said Timothy the Terrible. "You've poisoned me, you murdering bitch. You've killed me." He gagged most realistically.

Leeds's words died in his throat. He stood staring at Quarles. Then they both looked at the little woman who was sitting with her head in her hands.

They found Pedro Martinez, alias John Smith, in the cellar, lightly covered over with earth. His body contained nearly three grains of arsenic. Eve Addle spent the rest of her days in Broadmoor. There she told over and over again, to the boredom of the other inmates, the story of the way in which her happy married life had been ruined by the foolish mistake of moving to a new home in the unlucky month of October.

ALWAYS RATHER A PRIG

Margaret Yorke

"PRIMMY HAS COME to live near Whipton," said Daphne Blythe when she met Mildred Fisher in Fenwick's for lunch one day. Both were in town for a day's shopping, and they met like this two or three times a year. "We ought to do something about it."

"What?" enquired Mildred, and added, "she must be awfully old."

"Eighty next year—that's all. I used to think she was eighty then," said Daphne, and giggled.

Many years ago Mildred and Daphne had been pupils at St Wilhelmina's, where Miss Primrose ruled as headmistress. Most girls left St Wilhelmina's in those days equipped with the School Certificate, as it then was, a basic knowledge of the French language including some ability to speak it, a sound grounding in the Christian religion, and well mannered. Only a few went on to university, but some, in the brief years before marriage, were capable secretaries; others trained as nurses and therapists of various kinds. St Wilhelmina's had perished in the reign of Miss Primrose's third successor, worn down by rising costs and competition.

"We could have a party for her. Give her a good lunch somewhere. We could round up twenty or so old girls, couldn't we? I can think of several who live fairly near. I'm sure the old thing would enjoy it. We can't just leave her there, unacknowledged. And what else can we do? I don't know that Robert . . ." Daphne's voice trailed away.

She had been going to say that Robert, her barrister husband, might not be enthusiastic if Miss Primrose were asked to dine, and Mildred understood this. Her own Gerald would feel exactly the same.

"A hotel would be better than a hen lunch in one of our houses," she said, imagining the scene in her own. If that were to happen one might, perforce, get involved with other old St Wilhelminians; those who lived near enough might take to dropping in, want to use the swimming pool, and so on. It could lead to endless difficulties. Mildred's entertaining was mainly the kind that might lead to some sort of advantage. "I don't suppose she gets taken out to lunch very often," she added. "It's a good idea, Daphne. Have you got the last school magazine? We could round up some names from that."

So it was that in the next week twenty or so women, none of them young, who lived within forty miles of Whipton and who had been at St Wilhelmina's but had seldom or never met since, agreed to meet at a riverside hotel to feast their former headmistress.

"Who else is coming?" asked Naomi Kent.

Daphne read out the list of names.

"We'll all pay our own and I'll pay for Primmy," she said. "It should be quite fun. Have you kept up with anyone, Naomi?"

Naomi hadn't. She had been startled when Daphne announced her own identity on the telephone.

Daphne could not remember Naomi at all, apart from her name, but had discovered that she ran a bookshop in the area. A thin, dark girl, she thought, a few years younger than herself; Mildred had told her that.

"I could only come if it was a Wednesday," Naomi said. "I can't leave my shop very easily otherwise. But my assistant can manage for the last hour that morning."

By saying this she had expressed willingness to go to the luncheon. She must be quite mad, deliberately setting out to encounter that woman.

Daphne was saying that Wednesday was the best day for her too. Her Mrs Blossom came then.

Yes, and polishes the desk in Robert's study, hoovers the room where he sleeps with Daphne, cleans out his bath, thought Naomi.

She had never met the adult Daphne. The mental picture

she had of her lover's wife must be inaccurate, surely, after all these years.

None of this was her idea. She didn't want to stir things up. The fact that Daphne had included her in the scheme must prove that she had no suspicion.

The date was arranged, and on a July day Morris 1300's, Allegros, Minis, Ford Escorts, a Jaguar and a Bentley all converged on the riverside hotel chosen by Daphne for the entertainment of Miss Primrose.

To everyone's surprise, for all her pupils remembered her as tall and of a commanding presence, Miss Primrose was a thin little woman compared with her hostesses. Her white hair was bound round her brow with a snood of black velvet, as all remembered. Her face was quite rosy, for she was healthy and worked daily in her garden despite the torrid heat of that amazing summer.

She gazed round at the assembled women, all well into middle age. Daphne had supplied a list of those attending, which was thoughtful, for some of them Miss Primrose had not found memorable. Daphne, though, she remembered: captain of hockey and captain of tennis, but never head girl. She had once reported a junior girl for smuggling forbidden sweets into school; another time she had led a movement to ostracise a member of the fifth form who had, in Daphne's opinion, let down the school by forgetting her lines in the performance of *The Tempest* before the assembled parents.

What a dull, worthy bunch they were, Miss Primrose mused, sipping gin and tonic. The most interesting and successful of her former pupils were not free to entertain her thus, for they were too busy. There was a hospital matron; a senior civil servant; two doctors. The women here today were, most of them, conscientious wives and mothers who now, with their own families grown up, provided meals on wheels for the elderly, were kindly grandmothers, and pillars of Women's Institutes throughout the land: worthy and good. How bored their husbands must be. Of course, some were widowed, like Ruth Gibbs, brisk and smiling, now a part-time teacher; and Felicity Downes, who looked mournful still though her husband had died at least ten years ago and he had been both rich and stupid, so that her condition now must surely be improved.

Had she wasted her life, Miss Primrose suddenly wondered, eating trout. Had she kindled no spark in a single soul? Was there no woman here today who was witty and wise? Thinking thus, she agreed aloud with Hermione Curtis that her daughter should certainly profit by reading modern languages at the university and thought that perhaps she might grow out of dressing in garments only fit for rummage sales.

It was the daughters of these women who were the active ones, able to progress along paths hewn by the generations preceding them. And these were good women: Miss Primrose looked at their plump faces, all smiling benignly. "Do you remember?" they were asking one another, and talking of daring pranks like dormitory feasts and moonlight swims in the school pool. They were having a lovely time. Some might even meet again, after today. Impossible to imagine any of them in gym slip and aertex shirt.

One was different: Naomi Kent. For one thing, she had never married, but there had been some trouble. Miss Primrose fished the facts from her mind.

—Yes—she's had a baby—a daughter: In the war, it was, so the girl must be well grown by now, probably married and a mother herself.

"Let me see, Naomi—what are you doing now, my dear?" Miss Primrose boomed in the voice which had announced the school hymn, "Fight the good fight", at the start and end of each term.

"I run a bookshop, Miss Primrose," Naomi replied. Though over fifty, she was still slim and dark-haired.

"It's dyed," Mildred had whispered, and, "It's not, you know," Daphne answered, scrutinising the smooth jet strands.

"How interesting. And you're doing quite well in these difficult days?"

"Oh yes," Naomi said, though increasing costs and falling sales were a serious problem. She looked round at the plump, well-nourished women. Had any of them suffered as she had, felt joy and pain like hers? They all looked so smug, with their prosperous husbands or, in the case of the widows, their adequate pensions. She had never had any security. Even now, though Robert and she were together again after so many years apart, what if he died? No pension for her then. "Jemima —my daughter—is married now and she has a son," she said. Robert had always helped to pay for Jemima, but the girl did not know her father's name.

"How nice," said Miss Primrose, and the other ladies rustled in their seats. Fancy admitting to it! They'd heard rumours, of course, but hadn't really believed . . .

Daphne would not have invited Naomi, if she had known.

"Jemima?" she asked, frowning.

"My daughter," said Naomi, and longed to add, "and your husband's." Aloud, she went on, "Oh, I'm not married. It was thought a scandal then, when it happened, but nowadays no one turns away from an unmarried mother. Most of us have probably at one time or another mentally prepared ourselves in case it should happen to a daughter."

And these women would try to be understanding and tolerant if their daughters became involved with married men, she thought wryly.

Suddenly Miss Primrose recalled something that had bothered her. She had recognised Naomi before any of the other women, but it was not because she had changed less than the others. She had changed a lot—as a schoolgirl she had been quiet and shy, very unsure of herself, thin and plain. Now she had assurance, was slim but rounded, and she looked alive: she was the most alert-looking woman present. But more: Miss Primrose had seen her a few weeks before in a picture gallery with a grey-haired man who looked rather distinguished. They had not been paying much heed to the pictures, so rapt were they with each other, and this was what had struck Miss Primrose as unusual about them. It was rare to see a couple their age mutually so engrossed. She had assumed them to be husband and wife, but it seemed she was wrong.

Over coffee the photographs came out, and Miss Primrose admired families. Then her gaze was held fast. In one snapshot, smiling a little self-consciously, she recognised the man who had been with Naomi in the picture gallery.

"My husband Robert," Daphne was saying with pride. "He's a barrister—he gets some very big cases. He'll soon be a judge, I hope."

They walked by the river bank, later. It was hot. Insects buzzed about, and the noise of the weir made background distraction. Miss Primrose attempted to talk to the women she had been seated away from during lunch. Each treated her with the old deference; habit died hard.

Soon she found herself walking with Mildred Fisher.

"Tell me about Naomi," Miss Primrose instructed. "About her daughter—so unfortunate . . ." she tried.

Mildred might know the story.

"She was silly—got herself involved with a married man in some war-time escapade," Mildred said. "I heard about it from Betty Butts—she died, you remember. She was a friend of Naomi's."

There was a small silence out of respect for the deceased Betty Butts. Miss Primrose felt sad that some of her girls should not have survived their headmistress.

"He'd married some addlepate during the war, Betty said—the man Naomi got mixed up with. Very pretty but no brains. And he had to stick to her or she'd collapse. He became quite well known later on, I believe, though I don't know who he was. Betty seemed to think his empty marriage drove him on to success—he worked hard because his wife was dull and his home life uninteresting." Mildred paused in her recital. "Some women are very stupid," she declared.

"Had he legitimate children?" Miss Primrose enquired.

"Oh yes, so I believe," said Mildred. "I'd forgotten about it all until now—Daphne didn't mention that Naomi was coming. She can't have known anything about it—she seems a bit shocked. But then, she was always rather a prig."

She may be, and you're complacent, thought Miss Primrose, filled with dismay.

"I must talk to Naomi," she said, and the ranks of her girls eddied and flowed to allow this to happen.

"My dear Naomi, you look much younger than all your contemporaries," Miss Primrose informed her wayward pupil.

Naomi laughed.

"Perhaps I'm the only one here today who is her own person," she said. "The others are all performing the roles they think are expected of their husbands' wives."

"That's all that most of them are capable of," said Miss Primrose. "Though they are valuable citizens, I've no doubt. Good to their neighbours and excellent cooks. Home made jam and full freezers. You've had a hard time, Naomi."

"In some ways. I've put all that behind me long ago. Jemima is married—she's happy. I've had a lot of happiness too. And I can retreat into my solitude now when I close up the shop," said Naomi. "As you can, Miss Primrose. You always could, couldn't you? Being head must be lonely—it is, at the top of any concern. That's a compensation, isn't it, enjoying solitude?"

"That's true, my dear."

"And are you enjoying today? Seeing your girls, if you think of us still like that? Do we disappoint you?"

"I wish I could see some of the others—those who were too busy to come today. There were some with brains," Miss Primrose said wistfully. "You have brains, Naomi. You always had, though perhaps your school career was undistinguished."

"It was," said Naomi. "And I don't know about the brains. Perhaps. At least by using one's mind one can fight against grief."

"Yes," said Miss Primrose. "I hope we meet again after today, Naomi. You are one of St Wilhelmina's better specimens."

Naomi laughed.

"The others might not agree," she said. "They might say I was a disgrace to you and the school."

Dimly Miss Primrose remembered that first war. Dick had been killed on the Somme. She thought of his young, serious face as he asked her to marry him on his next leave. They had told no one of their plans, and there had been no next leave. She had gone up to Girton. After all this time she had almost forgotten, but not quite. Naomi, at least, had borne a child to her lover.

Miss Primrose thought about Robert Blythe. It was a good name for a judge. If he was so indiscreet as to meet Naomi where he might be recognised and fail to mask his emotions, he might never grace the bench.

"Daphne's children. Do you know what they're like?" Miss Primrose asked slyly. "What do they do?"

"The boy's a solicitor. The daughter's a Cordon Blue cook. They're both married," she said, and turned her brown eyes upon the faded but very alert blue ones of Miss Primrose.

"Children? Grandchildren for Daphne?" Miss Primrose pursued.

"Not yet. Expected, however," said Naomi, and then, a little maliciously, added, "They live some way away. They fear interference."

"I see," Miss Primrose nodded. "Thank you, my dear. Good luck with your shop."

Naomi, dismissed, drifted away and found herself next to Mildred.

"Funny old thing, Primmy, isn't she?" Mildred said. "I think she's enjoying her day. She's still spot on, though."

"Yes, she is," said Naomi. "Remarkable. But so many old ladies are like her, don't you find? Riding bicycles and mowing lawns. Tough."

"I wonder if we'll be as tough, if we live so long?" mused Mildred, rather surprisingly.

"Only the tough or the cossetted survive to great age," said Naomi.

Miss Primrose was ahead of them, walking with Daphne. The sun beat down on their two bare heads as they drew near to the weir, the white one with the velvet snood, and the grey one, old-fashioned lacquered set immovable, broad shoulders turned slightly to talk to the smaller old lady beside her.

No one saw how it happened. One minute the two were walking along the bank above the weir, conversing; the next, there was some sort of scuffle as Miss Primrose appeared to stumble. A cry rang out, then a real scream.

Daphne had gone, swept into the river and instantly over

the weir. By the time the others had rushed forward to look for lifebelts she had vanished.

It was Naomi who ran along the bank and found a boat which she paddled right up to the foot of the weir. But Daphne had disappeared.

Miss Primrose, apparently suffering from heat stroke, was taken to hospital where she spent the night. She recovered swiftly, and at the inquest on Daphne, whose body was washed up further down the river, said she had fainted. Daphne must have tried to prevent her from falling and in doing so had lost her own footing and slipped into the river which was notoriously dangerous there, above the weir.

A verdict of accidental death was recorded.

Six months later Miss Primrose read in *The Times* that His Honour Judge Robert Blythe had married Miss Naomi Kent, quietly, at Caxton Hall.

"One of my more deserving pupils, Naomi," Miss Primrose recalled. "And never a prig."

"WHAT YOU GAIN ON THE SWINGS . . ."

Jeffry Scott

"FASCINATING LITTLE PROBLEM," said Detective Sergeant Dix, who might have been talking to himself—but wasn't.

Little Mr Martin cupped a hand to his ear. "Shout up a bit, Sarge. This traffic . . ."

They were sitting in the lounge of Number Fifteen, a prime bit of 1930's jerrybuilding. Once the houses had been quite secluded, but that was before the arterial road appeared. Less than a hundred yards past Number Fifteen, the end house, the road sprouted abruptly, offering routes to several different parts of London.

Motorcycles whined and nagged, lorries grumbled and cleared their throats, cars yelled or made noises like canvas being ripped, according to age. Most vehicles had something in common: they left it far too late, deciding which of four streams to select, where the main road ravelled into strands.

Some drivers braked savagely, others went down through the gearbox. Practically everybody hooted at the fellow in front, ruddy roadhog.

"Sorry," Sergeant Dix acknowledged, in a modified shout. "I was saying, it's a fascinating problem."

"Only for you," Martin replied sadly. "Far as I'm concerned, 'tis an ordeal. Being innocent, and all . . ."

Dix stiffened in his overstuffed chair. Mr Martin, a well preserved if threadpapery sixty or so, had a face like crumpled washleather, all folds and creases, testifying to good humour as well as a troubled life. And Sergeant Dix could have sworn that Syd Martin had just . . . winked at him.

But now Syd was staring solemnly. Dix hoped that he had imagined the wink.

Nice room, he thought irrelevantly. Took him back to his young days, times of security and comfort. Bella Martin had been a shrew and a bully, but at least she hadn't banished the good feeling from this corner of the house.

Dust motes danced in shafts of sunlight spearing through the fake leaded windows, a ship in a bottle sailed on the mantelpiece, Syd Martin had his feet up on a stool and there was a formidable rack of pipes and a great jar of tobacco within arm's reach.

Dix's eyes narrowed. The pipe rack looked new and so did the pipes. Mrs Martin had vanished off the face of the earth—beneath it, more likely, the policeman reminded himself—three months ago.

"Things a bit cosier since she . . . left . . . eh?" he observed craftily. "Bit of a bachelor pad you've got here these days, Sydney."

"Can't say that I miss her," the other man agreed. "Still, she might come back." Suddenly there was no doubting the twinkle in his eye. Dix gave him back a boiled stare of disapproval. Not so deep down he sympathised with Mr Martin—his own wife was a little in Bella's mould—but the citizenry couldn't be allowed to go around killing off their partners. Apart from the legal aspect, it might start a craze . . .

"See here," Sergeant Dix began, and then thought twice about thumping the chair arm. Syd Martin had made himself snug in Number Fifteen, but dusting was not among his talents.

"I'll make us a nice pot of tea," Mr Martin struck in. "Seeing as we're to have a little chat. Don't get up, Sarge. Try a fill of my baccy—costs a bit more than average, but it's a lovely smoke."

"This isn't a flaming social occasion," Dix muttered, but Martin had pattered away to the kitchen. And it *was* good baccy. Guinea an ounce, probably. Syd could afford it, now that Bella wasn't there to swill and guzzle his income away.

Over the teacups:

"I'll be straight with you," Dix claimed. "Women Bella's age don't just disappear. That's a fact, Syd. All right, she was a bit disorderly in her habits—"

"Should have been had up long ago if you chaps were efficient," Mr Martin commented, without rancour. "If not for drunk and abusive, then prostitution."

Dix blinked at him. "Steady on, Syd. That's a bit strong."

"Speak no ill of the dead, you mean?" Mr Martin spent time guiding a tealeaf to the rim of his cup. "Well, I'm not admitting that she's dead. But you're right, I shouldn't have said that. Prostitutes do it for money, and Bella was more likely to pay her fancy men."

"You really hated her."

Mr Martin set his empty cup aside, filled an expensive straight-grain briar, and puffed luxuriously. "Past that dramatical talk at my time of life. Rather have Bella's room than her company, put it that way. I can't deny it. Honest as the day is long, me."

Sergeant Dix was aware of getting side-tracked. "Anyway, whatever her, um, hobbies may have been, Bella was no spring chicken, know what I mean? Set in her ways, like. Your sister-in-law and her old Mum are pestering us silly, and that's what they keep coming back to—Bella wouldn't just scarper. Not without contacting them."

A long, dribbling puff of smoke. "Bella might find that difficult, getting in touch."

Laughing at me, Dix mused. His cheeks reddened, he knocked his pipe out on the fender. Recognising a declaration of war, Mr Martin sat up straighter, though his eyes remained merry enough, among the wrinkles and creases.

Dix said: "This is where the problem comes in, Syd. For the sake of argument, we'll say you *have* killed her."

"Hypothetically," Martin suggested, helpfully.

"Okay, that too. So . . . you've done for her. What happened to the body? I've checked with your doctor. He says that sustained, violent effort would kill you, with that heart condition of yours."

Sergeant Dix became brutal. "Sustained, violent effort like lugging a corpse around, Syd."

Martin wagged his pipestem. "I'm not *that* much of an invalid, Sarge. If I take it slow but steady, you'd be surprised what I can handle. Well, the garden . . ." His glance through the window was sardonic.

"Sorry about that, but you did give us permission to dig," Dix mumbled.

Mr Martin shook a reproachful head. "I thought you'd trench it, give the soil a good airing. But it was more like the surface of the moon, by the time your lads finished. Talk about open-cast coal mining. Take me years to get it to rights again."

Sergeant Dix reminded himself that Syd Martin was no fool. The complaint had been more than a grumble; it was a gentle pointing-out that the police had checked Number Fifteen inside and out, never discovering so much as a lock of hair, a toenail, a fleck of blood . . .

"Then again, you couldn't have taken her far, in your state," Dix mused aloud. "And you don't have a car."

Martin chuckled fruitfully. "Don't even have a driving licence, Sarge." He jerked a thumb at the window, and the invisible yet all too evident road. "That lot, they do enough driving for me, thanks."

Dix realised that his ears had been filtering out the racket. Attention drawn, he winced at its sheer scale and nastiness.

Mr Martin interpreted the reaction. "Not so bad at night," he explained indulgently. "Peters out about midnight, then it can go for hours with hardly a sound. Anyway, I'm used to it, generally get a good night's sleep."

"Good for you," Dix commented sourly. " 'Course, you've got a clear conscience, eh? That helps you sleep like a babby, I suppose."

Choosing to misunderstand the taunt, Mr Martin agreed, "There's a lot off my mind these days. Bella was a trial, no two ways about it. Made me a laughing stock with her goings-on, and nagged me to death with her tantrums and throwing things and all that."

He caught himself, and the twinkle intensified. "Well, not quite to death, of course. *I'm* still here."

"Aren't you just." Sergeant Dix was grim. His masters had briefed him on the result of a conference that morning with the Director of Public Prosecutions. The D.P.P. disliked a murder charge without a body and—apart from slanderous suspicions from Mrs Martin's shiftless relatives—without evidence.

The police had been told, in effect, to go away and stop wasting the D.P.P.'s time, unless and until they found Bella's remains. Or unless and until Mr Sydney Kitchener Martin confessed to her murder. That would be splendid, the D.P.P. conceded. Otherwise . . . don't call us, sweetie, just leave your name at the stage door.

Mr Martin twitched his visitor back to the present. "Bella was a big woman, Sarge, strong as a man. How am I supposed to have done her in?"

"Funny you should mention that, Syd. Before you got that nice whack of compensation for the accident, you were doing a bit of light work for a year or two."

Closing one eye, Mr Martin affirmed, "Night watchman at Ferrazi-DeBezique."

Dix brooded in his chair. "Ferrazi's distribute drugs and chemicals, right? Enough poisons in their warehouse to kill off Britain, three times over."

Mr Martin nodded placidly. "I bet that's what they said when you asked them to run an inventory to see if—say a pinch of something, enough to do Bella's business for her—was missing! As near impossible to do, as makes no odds."

"Huh! Anyway, how you di—how it was done doesn't signify at the moment. I want to find that body. It can't be far."

Mr Martin swung his feet off the stool. "Hypothetically speaking, remember. I'm sure Bella is somewhere." He made a vague and totally unconvincing pass at his breast. "Nice to have a chin-wag, Sarge, but I'm a bit tired now and the Doc's warned me not to tax the ticker. See yourself out, will you?"

Sergeant Dix's car was parked in a lay-by on the far side of the main road, and having waited ten minutes and still been forced to take his life in his hands, dashing across, he could hardly hear himself think.

Sitting behind the steering wheel, he wasted a further minute disapproving of the neighbourhood.

It looked a right shambles. The local council had stopped

mowing the verges, since the energy crisis and rampant inflation had forced economies. So a metal stream, no, a cataract thundered between waving jungles of grass and weeds.

An idea struck him, There'd been a wheelbarrow in Syd Martin's garden shed, a big 'un, well oiled, fat wheeled, nicely balanced. Even Syd could have moved Bella's body a fair distance, in that.

For example, after dark, out of the house and across the garden and into the road. Being the last house, Number Fifteen was overlooked by only one next-door neighbour. Small risk, at night, when everybody would be glued to their TV sets.

But examination of the overgrown verge made Dix's theory wither. The grass was hardly two feet wide, no more than a narrow strip between concrete walls, designed to divide the houses' service road from the pavement. Not really room for a grave; further, Sergeant Dix's uncle was in the Borough Surveyor's department, and the sergeant remembered, suddenly, about the gas pipes.

They ran beneath this verge, rather than the service way or the main road. The idea was to make repairs easier without disrupting traffic. Syd Martin had lived here all his life. He must know that a grave above the pipeline decreed eventual discovery, when the Gas Board carried out inevitable maintenance or renewals.

"Nice try," murmured Sergeant Dix. Getting in his tinny little car, he fed himself into the cataract, allowed his metal chip to be swirled three-quarters of a turn about the roundabout, and headed for town.

He sensed that the Martin affair would remain a missing persons statistic and never be transferred to C.I.D.; destined for obscurity instead of a murder trial.

And Dix found himself unable to mourn over the likelihood. He'd seen Bella Martin in her prime, if that was the word. A nasty piece of work from any angle—especially her wretched husband's, he concluded wryly.

A few days later, Mr Martin was standing at the kerbside within sight of his home, staring out at the traffic.

Or rather, he was staring at what the traffic kept circling and spinning away from: the roundabout. A disc of grass enclosed in a concrete rim, a gently swelling dome a couple of feet high and perhaps twenty yards across.

It put him in mind of a modern riddle—what door is always open and always shut? A revolving door.

A roundabout was something the same: an island of no use in itself, created to define the sea of road. A desert island more desolated than Crusoe's.

Out on that island, a grave need be no more than inches deep—a matter of cutting and peeling the turf and scraping out the minimum of earth.

Even a handicapped, frail man could do it, given time and a trowel. Since the council had stopped cutting grass, he could lie there in cover and burrow away gently. Approaching cars would signal their presence by their headlights, half a mile before arriving.

After that it would be a matter of waiting beside the wheelbarrow, in the deeper shadow by the hedge, and picking the moment to trundle the flaccid, grotesque load across the road.

Mr Martin savoured smoke on his tongue, and expelled a long plume to mingle with the exhaust fumes. Unlike the majority of local people, he didn't detest the traffic. It was his ally.

Leaning on his stick, he considered what the doctor had told him that morning. He would be dead by the end of the year. Well, fair enough, at least the waiting time would be tranquil, even pleasurable.

Straining his eyes, he scanned the shaggy grass atop the roundabout. He hoped the council would go back to mowing it when money was less tight. The turf was well established again, they could start cutting whenever they pleased. Only he could detect a certain patch where the grass was a shade higher, a trifle greener.

If there was anything in talk of an after life, then he and Bella could argue the rights and wrongs of it at their leisure. . . .

For no clear reason, he remembered his first meeting with Bella, on the fairground at Hampstead Heath one bank holiday. She'd been younger and several stone lighter, of course. Possible, in those days, to mistake instability for vivacity, nagging for repartee. . . .

Mr Martin laughed shortly. What was the old saying? *What you gain on the swings, you lose on the roundabouts.*

"Well, I have," said Mr Martin to the uncaring traffic. And he went home to his tea.

TELL DAVID . . .

Penelope Wallace

I HAD BEEN married nearly three years when I first met the Blessingtons.

On the previous evening Tony and I had had a blistering row; these days we always seemed to be having rows. He was everything in the world to me and I loved him wildly, jealously and possessively. Yesterday he'd stayed late at the office and the dinner I'd so carefully cooked was dry and tasteless by the time we sat down to eat it. I was upset and he was irritable and he told me that if I "slaved over a hot stove" I was a fool; we had an *au pair*—I could have a full-time cook if I liked—and I had only myself to blame. I tried to explain that I wanted to do everything for him myself—that the *au pair* Yvonne had enough to do looking after young David . . .

So on this day I thought I'd take his advice. I left David with Yvonne and I drove over to Oxford and went to the cinema. The film was supposed to be a comedy but I suppose I wasn't in the mood for laughing. I nearly left at one stage, thinking that if I drove fast I'd be at home when Tony arrived; and then I thought that this was weakness and sat there wondering whether he was home yet, whether he was missing me, wishing he hadn't said those bitter things yesterday.

At last the programme ended and I made myself leave slowly—eight o'clock—I'd be home by nine, but perhaps Tony had been delayed at the office; I'd better have a meal first. I knew Oxford fairly well because Tony had been up at Oxford when I'd first met him—and I suppose, subconsciously, that was why I'd chosen to come here to the cinema, when there were many nearer to home.

I started to walk to a Chinese Restaurant where Tony and I

had often dined after the cinema. As I walked along the wide, tree-lined St Giles, I remembered how often we had gone this way and how happy we had been and I suddenly realised what a fool I was being. I thought of phoning and then decided to collect the car and drive straight home, and tell Tony that he was right and I was wrong—and hope that he'd forgive me.

I collected the car and drove out towards Henley. I hate driving in the dark and outside Oxford it began to get misty; and then the mist cleared but I realised I wasn't on the right road—in fact it was more of a lane than a road. It began to rain; the drizzle turned into a downpour and I couldn't even see a house where I could ask my way.

I drove along slowly and then, suddenly, there it was—a house standing on its own on a slight rise. I couldn't see lights from the windows but there was a drive which swept under a big covered porch, lit by two concealed floodlights; so there might be someone at home and I wouldn't get wet finding out. I drove in and as the front door came into the lights from my car, two more floodlights came on and I saw a light from inside over the front door.

I got out of the car and looked for a bell—I was still looking when a voice from nowhere said, "Can I help you?" I replied that I had lost my way.

"Come in," said the voice and the front door opened.

For a moment I was scared—it seemed like something from a horror film—but then I saw the brightly lit comfortable hall and I felt reassured. I stepped in and, from an archway on my left, a girl come forward. She looked about eighteen and she had a warm and friendly smile:

"David's searching for his map gadget," she said. "Won't you come in and have some coffee while he finds it?"

I followed her through the archway and sat down. The room was simply furnished with low chunky leather chairs and sofas. The light seemed to come from the walls and I noticed that there were no curtains—it puzzled me.

"One way glass," explained the girl, as she poured coffee from the low table. I helped myself to cream and sugar.

"Isn't it dangerous?" I asked. "Letting people in just because they say they're lost—I mean, I might have had a gang of armed men with me."

She smiled and pointed at the big television screen which hung on one wall.

"It's closed circuit TV," she explained. "The camera in the front porch is light and sound sensitive so we can see who is outside before we open the door."

It really was a fantastic house, all these up-to-the-minute inventions and yet the shape of the room and the archways gave it almost a Roman appearance—a perfect blend of old and new styles. I was looking at a further arch in the wall facing the window, when a young man came through. For a moment he was silhouetted against the brighter light in the room beyond and I nearly dropped my cup of coffee because, for a moment, I thought it was Tony. Then he came farther into the room and the illusion vanished. Tony was dark and neat and this boy was fair and untidy. It didn't surprise me to hear him say:

"Pat, I can't find the map gadget—I've looked everywhere."

He didn't look like Tony and yet his face did remind me of someone. I thought it was time I told them my name and where I wanted to get to; the room was so peaceful and they were so relaxed, I could have sat there for hours. . . .

David unfolded a rather battered old map of the district and explained how to get back on the main Henley Road. I'm not too bright with maps and finally I wrote it down. "First left; first left; first right; first right." I put the note in my coat pocket, finished my coffee and started to leave.

"You don't live very far away," said Pat. "Please will you come and see us again?"

I said I would love to, imagining it to be the usual social politeness.

"What about tea?" she asked. "Today's Thursday; can you come on Monday?"

I told her I would love to. They opened the door and waved to me as I drove down the drive and turned left.

I found the way quite easily but I couldn't get Pat and David out of my mind. I couldn't imagine why they'd asked me back. I was about five years older than Pat and, for women, that's a lot—particularly when one is only eighteen or so. I didn't feel that she was just being polite; perhaps they'd recently moved into the district and didn't know anyone; or maybe it was just politeness or kindness. I could always phone them—but I couldn't because at that time, I didn't know their surname and I'd no idea of their address.

When I got home it was nearly eleven. I told Tony what a fool I'd been the evening before and that I'd been a fool again to go to the cinema—but, for some reason, I didn't tell him about Pat and David.

The following Monday I set off on the road to Oxford—I'd noticed where I should turn off; first left, first left, first right, first right . . . and there I was again.

The house looked beautiful in the afternoon sunshine. I drove under the porch and this time Pat opened the door herself.

I followed her in and she explained that David would be back soon—he was fixing a friend's television. "He's terribly good with anything electrical," she told me.

And that, I thought, probably explains the gadgetry.

"I didn't realise he'd be at home," I told her. "I mean, I thought he'd be at work."

She looked surprised for a moment and then she replied: "Not on Mondays. They have a three day week."

Before I could comment, she asked me if I'd like to come upstairs and take off my coat.

I followed her up the shallow winding staircase. Again there were no doors; we went through an archway into the bedroom—again the low simple furniture and a big divan with a dark cover, and the same wall lighting.

"The bathroom's through there," said Pat. She waved at what I imagine was the only door in the house and I went in from curiosity as much as anything else.

Like the rest of the house, it was beautiful but functional and everything was greeny blue so that you felt you were in some deep sea cave.

I washed my hands and looked around for a towel: There wasn't one but, on the wall, a small rounded recess. I put my hands in and immediately warm scented air flowed around them. It was a sophisticated and more efficient version of the hand-driers I'd seen in some cloakrooms. In the corner was a rounded screen. I stood by it out of curiosity and, from this also, came the same warm air. Evidently for drying after the bath. It certainly cut down the laundry bills.

"It's a fascinating house," I told Pat as I followed her downstairs.

"I'm glad you like it."

And again I had this feeling that she wasn't being polite—she really was glad.

We sat down in the living-room and I was just about to ask her whether David had fixed all the gadgets in the house, when he came in—grinning broadly and accompanied by an extraordinarily beautiful girl.

"Hullo, Anita. Has David fixed it?"

"Perfectly," said the girl. "He is brilliant."

Pat asked her if she'd stay for tea but she murmured something about Mother getting anxious, gave us all a beaming smile and went out through a glass door to the garden. We heard the sound of her car starting up.

"Nice girl," said David, sitting down.

"No comment," said Pat, but she smiled at him as she went off to make the tea.

I knew how I'd have felt if Tony had been fixing televison for a girl as pretty as that. I also knew that I was wrong and that Pat's attitude was right.

David was speaking:

"Ann . . ."

I must have looked surprised . . .

"You don't mind being called Ann?"

I assured him that I didn't mind.

"Pat's a wonderful girl—you know, even these days, you get wives who are jealous; you don't always get the relationship we have."

I hadn't known that jealousy was supposed to be dying out and I was startled at his remarks—both of them seemed to speak from the heart without filtering their emotions through conventional channels.

"Some people have jealous natures," I told him, and at that moment Pat came in with the tea.

David asked me whether I had any children. "Pat and I plan to have a baby next year," he went on.

I told him that I had one son, David like himself.

"What's he like?"

"Well, he's fair, like me and he'll be two next week."

"Two," David repeated it like an incantation. "I remember my second birthday—at least I don't suppose I actually remember it, probably I was told afterwards what happened—this." He held out his left thumb and I could see a faint scar running just below the knuckle. "Apparently I picked up the cake knife and cut my finger instead of the cake—my mother got quite hysterical. It was soon after that . . ."

Pat put her hand on his arm:

"Please David, don't."

David looked at her and took her hand from his arm. His voice was curiously solemn:

"Ann and I were talking about jealousy," he told her, "and I've got to tell her—I've got to tell her that a person can lose everything they love, everything they value—just because they get jealous."

He turned to me.

"My mother adored my father, wildly, jealously and possessively and soon after my second birthday, she killed him—she thought he was in love with someone else. She killed them both —and before her trial she killed herself."

"How awful—and how awful for you. What happened to you?"

"There was a distant relation on my father's side. She looked after me and I took her name, Blessington." He gave me a crooked smile. "You see, Ann, why I hate jealousy."

I certainly did, and I began to feel terribly depressed. It was horrible to know that this woman had felt as I had felt and had taken such a terrible and irrevocable step.

I was really quite happy to leave.

As I was going, David said a strange thing:

"I have my mother's photograph—she was very beautiful."

Pat took me upstairs to collect my coat.

"Don't let David depress you," she said. "Please come again, and why not bring your David—we'd love to see him."

But I never did take David there.

I spent the next ten days remembering what David Blessington had told me and trying *not* to nag and *not* to ask Tony why he was late and where he'd been; but it was terribly difficult because I just can't be detached. Anyway Tony was getting home earlier and he'd promised that, on the Friday which was David's birthday, he'd really be back soon after lunch so that we could all have a birthday tea together.

I'd iced the cake myself and put on the two candles and placed it on the dining-room table. It was Yvonne's day off and I set the tea. Three o'clock came with no sign of Tony; at four o'clock I rang his office and they said he'd not returned since lunch and wasn't expected back that afternoon.

Young David started to shout for his tea so I took him into the dining-room—we'd just have to have our birthday tea without Tony.

I was just going to put David in his high chair when the phone rang. I ran into the hall. It must be Tony—it was.

"Ann—look I'm terribly sorry I got held up."

"I rang the office . . ."

"No, it wasn't that—I had lunch with Jane. You remember her—she's a second cousin."

I didn't remember. "When will you be here?" I asked him—and suddenly there was a terrible scream from the dining-room.

"Come soon," I told Tony. "I've got to go, it's David." I put back the phone, and turned to the dining-room. There was David standing in the doorway, clasping his thumb and blood streaming out. Oh God, I thought, the cake knife. I picked him up and carried him to the kitchen and held his thumb under the cold tap and saw how deep the cut was. I put a wet cloth on it, and carried him back to the telephone. I knew the doctor's number. He was at home. I told him what had happened and he promised to come straight over.

It seemed an eternity and I wished I hadn't hung up on Tony—if only he were here. David had stopped screaming but he was still sobbing and saying, "It hurts, Mummy."

At last the doctor arrived. He looked at David's thumb and dressed it, telling him he was a good brave boy. Then I heard Tony's key in the lock and I told him what had happened and the doctor assured us that it would soon heal and there would only be a slight scar.

"A scar just below the knuckle on the left thumb . . ." I said.

I could see the doctor looking at me anxiously. I felt as if my mind was one of those one-armed bandits, and one wheel had just clicked into place. Through the spinning of the others I could faintly hear the doctor talking to Tony and Tony replying, "Actually I've invited my cousin Jane down for the night—she's dying to see David." Then he looked at me: "I hope you don't mind, Ann, I was trying to tell you on the phone."

I tried to concentrate and I asked him what cousin.

"Jane," he repeated, "Jane Blessington . . ."

The wheels clicked into place and yet they were still turning in my brain, and all I could hear was the noise. I shut my eyes because there was so much I didn't want to see—

I can remember someone carrying me upstairs, and drawn curtains, and telling them about the scar and how little it showed. Then I was being told to "drink this" . . . later I remember opening my eyes and seeing a woman—she had a kind face.

"I'm Jane Blessington."

It was difficult to speak but I finally said it:

"Look after him—and give him that . . ." I pointed at the photograph of myself which stood on the dressing-table.

Jane tried to reassure me. She told me that Tony was fine and that I'd be better in a few days.

"Not Tony," I tried to explain. "David—tell him . . ."

But what could she tell him. I shut my eyes again. I think I slept and when I awoke, I tried to think. My mind seemed now like a frightened horse, always refusing that last jump.

I was vaguely conscious of Jane Blessington coming to say Good-bye, of the doctor giving me stuff to drink, of murmurs of "delayed shock", of Tony, of Yvonne bringing me milk drinks . . . but I knew that I'd got to take that final jump and face up to what lay on the other side, however frightening it was, I'd got to face it; so I went over in my mind everything that had happened from the moment I'd lost my way from Oxford. I tried to remember everything that had been said—and particularly everything that David had said. I remembered again his last remark: "I have my mother's photograph—she was very beautiful," and it gave me the courage I needed to admit that, somehow in some strange way, I had lost myself not only in direction but also in time.

David Blessington was my David—his scar was the one caused by my David cutting his finger on his second birthday. The house, the gadgets, they were all of the future. I had not known—but David had. He'd known that my name had been his and he'd had my photograph. So when he talked of jealousy, he'd been warning me. When he'd told me that I'd killed Tony . . . No. That couldn't be the answer. I'd never kill my beloved Tony; it must have been just a dream, a kind of warning. . . .

The next time Tony came in, I asked him to get my blue coat from the wardrobe.

"Is there a note in the pocket?" I asked.

He put his hand in and drew out a paper.

"What does it say?"

"First left, first left . . . it looks like directions."

"It is. Please give it to me."

He looked puzzled but he put it in my hand. I read it myself —so it wasn't a dream; there were those simple directions which told the way from the Blessingtons' house to ours—and equally from our house to theirs.

"Please Tony, sit down, I've got to tell you something."

He sat on my bed and I told him everything.

I could see that he didn't believe a word . . .

"Ann, dear, you've been ill . . ."

"Then what about the note?"

"You could have written that at any time. Look, you said they had a telephone."

"Yes, I noticed it."

"Then we'll look in the telephone directory."

"They won't be in it."

Tony picked up the bedside extension and dialled Directory Enquiries. They had no Blessingtons in the district.

"You see?" he said.

"No," I told him, "I don't see. Don't you understand it was —oh I suppose nineteen-ninety-eight or nine, their number wouldn't be in this year's directory. Tony, you're not in love with anyone else are you?"

"No, I am not."

I could see that the question annoyed him.

"It may be a warning," I tried to explain. "Maybe I can stop it happening. I do love you so much, Tony."

"I love you, too. Now you must get some sleep." He kissed me gently.

"Tony," I called after him. "That gun, please put it somewhere else. Don't keep it in the drawer—please, Tony."

He called out "goodnight" and I turned off the light and tried to sleep. It looked as though I'd got to fight it out alone —I'd got to fight. . . .

The next day I felt stronger—it was going to be all right. It was a warning and I was never going to be jealous again. I trusted Tony absolutely—I wasn't going to be possessive, either. . . .

That evening the doctor said I could get out of bed and sit by the window. I sat by the window and watched the sun set, and I felt at peace.

The next day I was up for longer.

"Tomorrow you can come downstairs," the doctor promised.

I sat by the window and wished that Tony would come up. Then I tried walking about the room and I thought I would give him a surprise.

I went quietly down the stairs and into the living-room. It was empty. I tried the dining-room; he wasn't there but I could see light from under the kitchen door. He must be in there, cooking something special to surprise me.

I opened the door. . . .

Tony was in the kitchen—and so was Yvonne—and he was kissing her. Kissing her with a passionate intensity. My Tony, my Tony—he wasn't mine any more. And I was standing right beside the desk where Tony kept his gun.

As I opened the drawer, half of me was praying that he'd done what I asked him and that he'd moved the gun—but he hadn't, and as I felt it cold in my hand, I was glad.

So little had he cared, I thought, as I raised the gun and fired—twice.

. . . Jane Blessington has taken David and she will get his name changed to hers. "But I won't pretend I'm his mother," she told me—she's very like Pat, the same serenity, I suppose that's why he chooses her for his wife.

The trial is next week.

I shall use my time wisely, for, as David said, his mother killed herself before the trial—

I had my chance and I didn't take it; yet perhaps I am fortunate, for I have no worry about David. I know that he will be happy, that he will be all that I could hope for and I know Pat will be a wonderful mother—to my grandchildren, and I know that she will never be jealous . . .

I know, too, that David has forgiven me—he said I was beautiful.

MURDER IN MIND

James Pattinson

WHEN I PASSED Simpson's house on my way to the office a couple of workmen were carrying a large galvanised iron tank up the garden path. The thought flashed into my head in an instant: He means to drown his wife in that tank! And it gave me a tingling sensation in the spine, and a bit of a kick too if the truth must be told, because it isn't often you see a man making preparations for a murder.

Simpson was there directing the workmen. He was one of those thin, bony characters who look as though they never get enough to eat. He was gloomy too, always apparently expecting the worst to happen. If the sun was shining he would say it was too good to last, and if it was raining he would maintain that it had set in for the week.

His wife was entirely different. She was a large, cheery woman with one of those cackling laughs that make sensitive persons shudder all the way down to their toes. Maybe it was the laugh that annoyed Simpson; perhaps he hated seeing anyone so obviously enjoying life while he could see in it nothing but wretchedness and misery. I don't know. What I do know is that he detested the sight of Mrs Simpson and was always talking about how he would do her in one of these days.

"She's got it coming to her," he would say. "It's only a matter of time before I put her away for keeps. I've stood it long enough, and that's the truth."

Which was why I had this idea when I saw the tank.

Maybe he means to fill it with sulphuric acid and let the acid eat her away and then run her out through the tap, I thought. I wonder whether he's remembered about the false teeth.

I'd read about things like that, you see, and I knew that false teeth were resistant to acid.

Simpson noticed me and gave a brief, jerky nod. "It's going to rain. Mark my words, there'll be a downpour before long."

"You may be right," I said. And then: "Have you thought about the false teeth?"

He didn't seem to get it. Or if he did he pretended not to.

"I haven't got false teeth," he said. "Man and boy I've had these ones for close on fifty years and they're still sound. I never ate sweets, see? It's the sweets that do 'em in. If I had my way, I'd make sweets illegal."

And I imagine he would have done so too, because it would have been a way of hitting at the kids, and he couldn't abide kids any more than he could abide his wife. He hadn't got any of his own and he didn't think anyone else ought to have any either. It crossed my mind that perhaps he intended drowning a few of them as well as Mrs Simpson. The tank looked big enough.

The workmen had come to a halt and Simpson growled at them for slacking; so they got a move on again and the last I saw of the tank it was disappearing round the corner of the house with Simpson following it.

I gave him a final warning. "The coppers will identify the teeth. Dentists always recognise the teeth they've made. People have been hanged by a set of choppers."

But he wasn't listening. He was telling the men not to step on the flower beds or knock the paint off the window sills; which for a man who had decided to do in his ever-loving wife was being a bit pernickety in my opinion.

When I got home that evening I told Mabel that Simpson had bought a tank to drown his wife in. It seemed the kind of thing she ought to know.

Mabel looked at me with those innocent blue eyes of hers and I could see that she didn't believe a word of it.

"How do you know?" she said.

"I saw the tank being carried in by a couple of honest British workmen."

Of course, I didn't really know whether they were honest or not, and they might even have been Southern Irish if it came to that; but I was giving them the benefit of the doubt.

This failed to satisfy Mabel. I must say she takes a lot of

convincing. "I'm not denying you saw the tank," she said, "but how do you know he's going to drown his wife in it?"

"It stands to reason," I said.

She still wasn't buying it. "I can't see how he would get her into it. She's a big woman and he doesn't look very strong. If it comes to that, I don't even think you could lift me into a tank."

I resented this. It was an aspersion on my manhood. "I could do it easily," I said. And I picked her up just to prove the point. Which would have been all right if my disc hadn't slipped again and ruined the demonstration.

"Anyway," I said, when she had helped me on to the sofa, "he'll probably drug her first and rig up some kind of block and tackle on the beams."

"What beams?" Mabel asked.

"The beams in the shed where he's got the tank, of course."

"If he's got it in a shed."

I was a bit nettled at this. It seemed to me that she was doing her best to be obstructive. Besides which, the disc was hurting.

"Of course he's got it in a shed; otherwise how would he rig up a block and tackle?"

"The whole thing's only a theory," Mabel said.

Which is just like a woman—illogical.

Simpson was in his garden again when I went past next morning. The sun was shining and there wasn't a cloud in sight.

"It's going to rain," he said. "I can feel it in my bones."

"What have you done with the tank?" I asked.

"It's in the shed at the back of the house. I got it for the wife."

"That's what I thought," I said.

"It'll keep her out of my sight."

Well, that was one way of putting it. He was certainly being very brazen about the whole affair, but that was like Simpson.

"It's for her to dye in," he added.

"Oh, yes," I said. "Of course. To die in."

"She's going to dye that wretched cloth she's been weaving."

"Oh," I said. But he didn't fool me for a moment. I could see he had regretted admitting so much and was trying to cover up. No woman would have wanted a tank as big as that to dye her home weaving in. It was a thin story, to say the least.

"Well, don't forget the false teeth," I said.

He gave me a look, as though he thought I was a bit funny in the head. "I don't know why you keep talking about false teeth. You must have dentures on the brain."

That evening I told Mabel what I had found out. "It's just as I thought. It is in the shed."

"And has he got a block and tackle?"

"I didn't ask him. But he must have. It stands to reason, doesn't it?"

"Not if he doesn't intend to kill her."

"But of course he intends to kill her. He's always said so."

"People who intend to kill their wives don't go round making a song about it."

"How do you know? Have you ever met anybody who intended to kill his wife?"

"No," she said. "But it stands to reason."

As I said before, women are illogical.

On the third morning after the arrival of the tank I noticed that the Simpsons' milk bottles had not been taken in. It looked ominous to me. The bottles were still on the doorstep when I returned in the evening.

"I think he's done it," I said to Mabel. And I told her why.

"If you think that," she said, "you'd better call the police."

I considered this suggestion and came to the conclusion that there was no reason to be hasty. Nothing I did now was going to save Mrs Simpson if the deed had in fact been done, and I have always been a shade chary of contact with the forces of law and order.

"You're scared," Mabel said.

I corrected her with some dignity. "Nothing of the kind. I am merely exercising reasonable caution."

"You could at least go and see if there's anyone at home."

I knew there wouldn't be. Simpson had probably done the job during the night and had slipped away under cover of darkness.

As likely as not he was out of the country long ago, on his way to South America with a false moustache and dark glasses.

All the same, there was no harm in making sure, so I went round to the house and rang the front door bell. As I had expected, there was no answer. I rang it again and then went home.

"No one," I said.

"I think you had better go to the police," Mabel said.

"I thought you didn't believe he intended killing her."

"I still don't believe it. But burglars may have broken in and tied them both up. May even have killed them. It's your duty to call the police."

When she put it like that I didn't see how I could avoid it. So I put on my bowler hat to show them that I was an honest man and a pillar of society and went along to the station.

I must say they were very polite. They listened with great attentiveness to what I had to say, and though they didn't immediately put the case in the hands of a detective inspector or even a detective sergeant, they did send a uniformed constable back with me to the scene of the suspected crime.

"You realise of course, sir," the desk sergeant said, "that there may be a perfectly innocent explanation. Mr and Mrs Simpson may just have gone away for a few days."

"But the milk bottles—"

"People sometimes forget to warn the milkman. They shouldn't, but they do." He sighed. "It's one of the weaknesses of human nature with which we have to contend."

I must admit I felt a trifle self-conscious walking back with the constable. Well, it's not the usual thing, is it? Not for one who has led a blameless life. I kept at a reasonable distance from him so that people could see there were no handcuffs connecting us, and I was relieved when we got to Simpson's house without meeting anyone I knew.

Of course the constable insisted on ringing the bell, though I told him he was wasting his time. Then he tried the door, but it was locked; and then we went round to the back.

The back door was locked too, but the shed door wasn't. I pushed it open and the first thing I saw was the tank. It was stood up on some brick piles so that I couldn't see into it. but I looked up at the roof and there was no block and tackle. I guessed that Simpson had dismantled it after use or had employed some other method.

I warned the constable to mind the acid on his clothes, and he said: "What acid?" The police can be very obtuse when they set their minds to it.

"That tank," I explained, "is full of concentrated sulphuric acid and Mrs Simpson's body is in it."

The constable said that in his opinion I had been looking at too much television, but to humour me he fetched a box and we both stood on it and peered over the rim of the tank.

I had been quite wrong. There was no acid in the tank and no Mrs Simpson slowly decomposing. Instead there was a lot of blue dye and Mr Simpson looking even more blue than usual.

I saw then why there had been no block and tackle. Mrs Simpson was a well built, vigorous woman and Mr Simpson had never weighed very much. She had probably found it comparatively easy to lift him into the tank.

"I think I had better go and ring the station," the constable said. I thought he was looking a trifle green, but it could have been the effect of the light.

Mabel crowed when I told her the gruesome details. "I told you that nobody who intended killing his wife would go round telling people so."

"How do you know he didn't intend killing her?" I said. "She may simply have forestalled him."

Mabel gave me a long, cool stare with her innocent blue eyes and admitted that I could be right. "And you can't really blame her, can you?" she said. "If I'd been in her shoes I should have done exactly the same."

Now that is the kind of remark that's calculated to make a man think. The result of my thinking was that I went round to the ironmonger's and cancelled an order for a tank. Of course I have implicit faith in Mabel, but it's as well to be on the safe side. You don't want to throw temptation in people's way, do you?

SCENT OF LILAC

Judy Chard

IT MAY SEEM strange that such a sweet perfume as that of the lilac blossom should fill me each succeeding spring with cold horror, and a sickening creeping of the flesh, for it all happened such a long time ago—nearly 30 years this May, in fact.

It was the custom in those days at the end of school term for the long-legged, dowdy girls, who attended boarding schools on the south coast, to be escorted across London by some relative or friend, in the event of their having to catch a homeward bound train at another station.

My escort was always Uncle Robert. He loomed like some nebulous monster at the end of the journey.

I couldn't put my feelings about Uncle Robert into words; to everyone else he seemed a kindly and benign old bachelor. Only I knew instinctively that there was something wrong—something to be feared. He made the ends of my nerves tingle with revulsion.

He was really my great uncle—Gran's brother. He and his other sister, Rose, lived in Launceston Gardens, Kensington. Sometimes I spent a few days of my holidays with them, sharing Aunt's bedroom in the prim Victorian house, its front windows looking out over the gardens which gave the Square its name. These were seedy to my country eyes—a few privet bushes, some sooty lilacs, which never struggled into blossom, and straggly grass surrounding a seat whose green paint was chipped and blistered.

Precisely at eight each morning Walker, the maid, would bring Aunt's tea, with a small cup for me on the tray, and a plate of thin bread and butter.

The garden at the back of the house was not much more than

a glorified yard, a lawn surrounded by flower beds, flanked by high walls, two gravel paths edged with shining kidney-shaped stones, and the big lilac tree, whose heavy purple blossom perfumed the May breeze.

At the end of one of these paths was a small brick building, once used for tools and bric-a-brac. Now it housed Uncle Robert's photographic equipment, his dark-room, and a number of felt-covered boards which displayed his collection of photos, taken during his travels all over the world, and, more recently—portraits of young girls.

Each picture, whatever its subject, had one common element—it portrayed perfect, unsullied beauty, captured and frozen forever by the camera.

At some time during my visit I would have to accompany him to this studio, as it was called, to see the latest additions to his collection. In his absence it was forbidden territory. It was curious that this harmless small building should have been the focus of my feelings of fear, and revulsion of Uncle Robert.

With his hand resting on my shoulder, he would take me from study to study, explaining—absorbed—as though it were an audience and not a ten-year-old child he addressed.

He would quote Keats, "A thing of Beauty is a Joy forever". "At least it should be," he would add, "providing man does not tamper with it. Here, anyway, it is preserved and held in its perfection, unsullied by age, indulgence, or mood."

This was all rather above my ten-year-old head, but, somehow, I was glad he never wanted to photograph me, thankful my features were too ugly to preserve for immortality.

He would look down at me sadly, "A pity you are so plain, child." He stooped and kissed my cheek, his drooping moustache tickling my mouth, and a choking panic would rise in me. I drew away, pretending to examine some particular photograph, my skin prickling with goose-pimples.

It was on one of these occasions that I noticed Alice.

I gave the girl in the portrait this name because I had recently fallen under the spell of Lewis Carroll's character. I thought the drawings of her quite beautiful, the pale hair held back by a ribbon from the flawless, oval face.

This photograph could have been her. It was larger than usual, and hung alone.

"Who's that?" I asked.

"Oh—just a girl—no one special." He sighed, and added as though to himself, "but to me her face is the personification of beauty and purity."

At that moment Aunt called us for tea, and with relief I burst into the fresh air and tore up the path as though pursued by a demon, drinking in the warm summer scent of the lilac.

At the end of the winter term Uncle Robert saw me across London as usual. We had an hour to spare and went to the Zoo.

It was there I saw Alice.

I tugged his arm and pointed her out.

He pretended not to see her. She turned away when she saw me, but I saw a flicker of recognition in the enormous blue eyes as they rested on Uncle Robert.

Christmas passed, and the spring term. Uncle Robert had gone on one of his photographic tours and Walker, the maid, met me, and took me back to Launceston Gardens for lunch before I was put on the train for Kent.

Aunt Rose sat straight as a ramrod in her winged chair. The folded fan of paper and jar of pampas grass were in the grate—sure signs of approaching summer; the french windows were open to the sunlit lawn. She kissed my cheek and dismissed me to the garden until lunch was ready.

The lilac filled the air with such a weight of perfume that it was almost tangible.

On impulse I went to the white painted door of the studio.

I glanced over my shoulder. No one was about. Somehow the place had lost its air of menace with Uncle Robert absent.

I turned the handle and went in.

Here it was peaceful, the hum of traffic remote. A bluebottle buzzed in a cobweb at the window. There was a funny smell—musty and rank—hanging in the air.

The beautiful pictures were in their places, except for the one of Alice.

I began to search the neat piles of paper on the shelves. Negatives, tissue paper, envelopes, mounting squares all tumbled on to the floor.

At the very bottom of the shelf, bent in half so that the beautiful face was distorted, was the photo of Alice.

Someone had put an enormous red cross through it and printed a four letter word I didn't know across her mouth. Quickly I put everything back as I had found it.

As I rose to go I noticed the door to the dark-room was ajar.

My curiosity aroused, I pushed it open and a shaft of sunlight from the window behind me shone through the dancing motes of dust on a silk stockinged leg and high heeled shoe.

I threw open the door to its full extent.

Alice lay on her back on the floor. A heaving, crawling mass of buzzing flies covered her neck and wide blue eyes, . . . the golden hair was a tangled, bloody mess about her head.

I felt physically sick and the sunlit room rocked and swayed in a giddy circle. I put my hand against the door to steady myself.

At that moment I heard Walker calling me to lunch.

I don't remember getting back to the house. I went to the tiny cloakroom in the hall and was sick. The reek of the dark-room, mingled with the perfume of the lilac, stuck in the back of my throat. I was terrified that the horror of the scene, and the guilt of my invasion of forbidden territory, would show on my face.

I struggled through lunch, pleading a headache. It was with immense relief that I left the house with Walker to catch my train. The fresh air in the spring-warmed streets cleared my head.

When the body was eventually discovered the press went to town on the sordid details of Uncle Robert's crime.

"Alice" was a nursemaid called Edna Harper. Uncle had cut her throat with one of the knives he used for trimming photographs.

No one had seen him take her to the studio, and there seemed no motive for the murder. It wasn't even his baby she was going to have—at least half-a-dozen men came forward and said they had been her lovers.

But his own counsel couldn't get Uncle Robert to say anything in his own defence—all he did was mumble some lines from Keats:

"She cannot fade, though thou hast not thy bliss
"Forever wilt thou love and she be fair . . ."

They put him in a mental home where he died soon after.

But of course I've never been able to explain to anyone why I can't live in a house with lilacs in the garden . . .

"YES, SIR: NO, SIR"

John Rossiter

DETECTIVE CHIEF SUPERINTENDENT Inkbarrow disliked snow. He disliked anything that came between him and his use of metalled and asphalted roads or the civilised necessity of cement footpaths. For the past two days snow had been falling in huge feathery gobbets, laying its pall of cold whiteness impartially on the city and on the surrounding moors.

Having driven perilously from his office on four rubber tyres that slithered and skated on icy slush with the minimum of adhesion, Inkbarrow was in no mood to do anything but stay indoors after the eating of his solitary dinner. A thick-set man with the beginnings of a middle-aged belly concealed by the well cut suit he wore, he possessed the touchy irascibility of an incompetent widower coping not very successfully with the feminine problems of cooking and bed making.

As he poured tonic water into his gin glass the telephone bell rang from the hall. He said "Damn!" and took the glass with him, placing it handy on the shelf on which the telephone handset stood. Through the door he could see flakes of snow drifting into the light from the black sky and melting on its pebbled glass.

"Yes?" he said into the mouthpiece. A draught blew in from under the door. He scowled and shivered. It was cold in the hall and he was in no mood to be amiable.

It was the Headquarters Operations Room Inspector. "Sir, will you please telephone P.C. Ockley at Upper Howick 226. He's at Doctor Roath's house and Doctor Roath has been murdered."

"How?" Inkbarrow could take this kind of information with all the professional phlegm of having dealt with murder and violent death for nearly thirty years.

"I understand he's been badly beaten about the head in his house, sir. I haven't any other details. P.C. Ockley was a little, er, incoherent."

"Right." He eyed the gin and tonic morosely. Investigating a murder, he was fond of pontificating to his men, was much like going to bed with a woman: best done stone cold sober. "Lay on for the Chief Constable and the Deputy Chief to be told. Get hold of the pathologist. Also Chief Inspector . . ."

"Sir!" Inspector Walton cut across his instructions. He knew the drill for murder anyway. It was all recorded and sellotaped to the wall of the Operations Room.

"Yes? What is it?" Inkbarrow didn't like being interrupted either.

"The road's blocked, sir. We can't get through. Nothing can."

"Oh? So what am I supposed to do?" he asked unreasonably. "Wait for it to clear itself?" Upper Howick was fifteen miles away and in the middle of the nowhere-else-to-go Wesdale Moor.

"I'm sorry, sir." Inkbarrow had made it the Inspector's fault. "The latest report says the B6306 leading to it is blocked with twelve-foot drifts. . . ."

"All right, all right," he said testily. "I get the message. After you've told the Chief, get hold of the City Engineer and have a snowplough organised. Then send a radio car to me for a communications link."

He depressed the studs, cutting himself off, then dialling Upper Howick 226. While he waited an answer he thought of Ockley.

Inkbarrow knew him fairly well. Which was not the case with every young constable in the county. He was a pale-faced ineffectual lad who wore an earnest expression and worried a lot about his inability to cope. And with reason, Inkbarrow considered. He had been given a trial run on the C.I.D. as a plainclothes aide, proving himself more fitted to wear uniform, to fret about swine fever outbreaks and straying cattle in the septic tank areas rather than dealing with the sophisticated villains of the city. But he came to mind just as readily because of his wife; before her marriage a local Miss Punch Tape Operator 1968 or something similar. She possessed unsettlingly large breasts and had stirred up disciplined and almost forgotten lusts at the last Police Ball. He knew it was as well that Ockley had been posted to the relatively unpopulated quiet of Upper Howick.

A wall mirror hung near the telephone. Thinking of the breasts he licked his lips and regarded his reflection with some satisfaction. Fifty-three wasn't senility. He had all his own teeth—he bared them to reassure himself of their whiteness—and his hair had survived the bleaching of time, retaining its black crispness. Some young women liked their men older; experience making them more understanding, more sensitive to a woman's needs.

The voice that answered his calling was typically hesitant.

"P.C. Ockley?"

"Yes, sir." Inkbarrow's voice needed no introduction and Ockley; fifteen unapproachable miles away, sounded as if he were standing rigidly to attention.

"Right. What's the trouble, Ockley?"

"Doctor Roath, sir. I think he's been killed." He was clearly on the edge of panic at the situation in which he found himself.

"So I understand," Inkbarrow said calmly. "You're there with him?"

Ockley swallowed. "Yes, sir."

"All right, Ockley. You're sure he's dead?"

"Yes, sir."

"We wouldn't know by whom, I suppose?"

"No, sir."

"What sort of an injury has he?"

Ockley swallowed again. It came magnified over the telephone as a soft *glop*; as if his Adam's apple had dislocated itself. "He's pretty badly hit about, sir," he said reluctantly. "On his head and face. There's blood and stuff . . ."

"You're *sure* he's dead?"

"Yes, sir."

"Would you know for how long?"

"No, sir."

"You couldn't guess?"

"No, sir."

Inkbarrow was dangerously quiet for a moment. "Can I assume he isn't decaying, Ockley? Nor even stiff as a board?"

"No, sir. I mean, he isn't . . . he hasn't been dead very long."

"How long is long to you, Ockley?"

"Poss . . . possibly an hour, two hours . . ."

"Good. Why not bloody well say so in the first place instead of wasting my time?"

"Sir, I . . ."

Inkbarrow cut across his explanation. "Is there a weapon?"

"No, sir."

"You're sure there's nothing about that could have been used, Ockley? A poker or something similar?"

"There's a poker, sir, but . . ."

"Agh!"

". . . but I think it's too light, sir. Too flimsy."

"Then why mention it, Ockley?" Inkbarrow said sharply. "Please keep to the point."

"Yes, sir."

"It's queer . . ." Inkbarrow was musing aloud. "No," he said, shaking his head. "It wouldn't strike you."

"What, sir?"

"That whatever was used the murderer took away with him."

"Whatever was used, sir?" Ockley echoed feebly.

"The murder weapon, Ockley, the murder weapon. The first thing you look for." He eyed his gin and tonic with a growing frustration. It was tempting. Particularly as an antidote against the depressing knowledge that the thick, slow-thinking Ockley was the only man at the scene; that he had to use a rural constable's deficient and untrained senses as his own eyes and ears and nose. He lifted the glass and took a quiet sip from it. "Now listen, Ockley," he said carefully as if speaking to a backward schoolboy. "Start from the beginning. Omit nothing. Paint the picture as you see it. You understand?"

"Yes, sir."

"Where are you telephoning from? Where in the house?"

"From his lounge, sir."

"Describe what you see."

"It's a very big room, sir. There's a settee and three easy

chairs and a sideboard thing. And lots of books, sir. A rolltop desk that's open. . . ."

"You bloody idiot, Ockley! The body!" Inkbarrow barked at him.

"Yes, sir. I'm sorry, sir. I thought you meant . . ."

"Describe the body, Ockley, for Christ's sake and don't waffle. Its position; its condition."

"Yes, sir."

Inkbarrow used Brown Rappee snuff. He withdrew a small lacquered box of it from his waistcoat pocket, flipped the lid open with a thumbnail and pushed the powder into his nostrils, sniffing. "All right," he said impatiently. "Get on with it."

"Doctor Roath's lying on his back on the carpet near his desk, sir. His feet are under it. His . . . his head is near the chair. Sir . . . sir, he's got no trousers on. . . ."

"*No trousers!* You mean he's undressed?"

"Yes . . . I mean no, sir. He's got his jacket on . . . his other clothes. His shoes, sir, are by his side."

Inkbarrow frowned at his reflection. "He's exposed?"

"I'm sorry, sir?"

"Oh, Christ!" He raised his eyes to the ceiling. "Is he showing his equipment? His genitalia?"

"No, sir. He's quite decent."

"Is there anything else about him that's unusual?"

"I . . . I don't think so, sir," he faltered.

"Ockley, for God's sake use the brains you're supposed to have. Give me *facts*. Describe things."

"The shoes, sir," Ockley said desperately. "Brown with elastic inserts. A tweed jacket, green and brown colour. His shirt's fawn with a brown knitted tie. Brown socks. His underpants are blue nylon, sir."

"Is there blood on any of it?"

"Yes, sir. On the jacket and shirt. And . . . and his teeth, sir. Some are on the carpet . . . ."

"Where on the carpet?"

"Near his head, sir."

"But no trousers?"

"No, sir."

"And that means nothing to you?"

"I don't think so, sir."

"They're not in the room?"

There was a short silence and Inkbarrow could imagine Ockley's bovine eyes searching around. The man was going the right way to give Inkbarrow an ulcer.

"I think they're on the fire, sir. There's an unburned piece of cloth in the hearth . . . ."

"Is the fire still burning?"

"Yes, sir. Not much though: more smouldering. I can see the zip still attached to the material, although it's all black."

"Don't touch it, Ockley. It'll stay like it is without interference." He thought about the fact of the trousers for a few seconds. "Would you know why they were burned, Ockley?"

"To . . . so we wouldn't find them, sir?"

"Brilliant, Ockley. But *why*?"

"Because there's blood on them, sir?"

"Don't be stupid. It's also on his jacket and shirt, isn't it?"

"Yes, sir."

"And *they* haven't been burned."

"No, sir."

"Is there anything in his hands?"

"No, sir."

"Are you guessing or have you looked?"

"I looked, sir. They're opened."

"No defensive marks?"

"I'm sorry, sir?"

"Defensive marks, Ockley. If someone's attacking you, wouldn't you try and stop him? Ward off the blows with your hands and arms?"

"I didn't see any, sir . . . *Prince! Come away*!"

"Who the hell was that, Ockley? Who are you talking to?"

Ockley's voice faltered. "Prince: my dog, sir. He was sniffing at the bit of cloth in the hearth. . . ."

There was a moment of stupefied silence. Then Inkbarrow exploded his outraged anger into the mouthpiece. "*Ockley!* Are you telling me you've brought your bloody dog inside with you? Allowed it to trample all over the scene of a serious crime! A murder! Probably pissing over everything likely to give us a clue . . . ?" His voice rose to a shout, vibrating the instrument he held in his hand. "GET HIM OUT, OCKLEY, YOU BLOODY HALF-WIT! AT BLOODY ONCE!"

He waited, his hand holding the receiver shaking with the fury he was unable to stopper down. He drank from his glass of gin and tonic, fuming at the man's incredible stupidity; at the probable loss to the Forensic Laboratory chemists and physicists of vital evidential fibres, hairs and dusts. And all by this blundering oaf of a constable and the cross-grained fate that left him alone and unsupervised at the scene. Snowflakes were still drifting against the glass of the door and he turned away from them. Snow and Ockley in combination were almost too much.

"Sir?" Ockley was back, sounding wooden-lipped, armed against the anticipated anger of his senior.

"Listen to me, Ockley." Inkbarrow tried hard to keep his words under control. "You were attached to the Department long enough for anybody but a cretinous mental case to understand the necessity of keeping the scene of a crime isolated. Completely and absolutely isolated."

"Yes, sir, but . . ." He did his little *glop* noise again.

"There's no damned 'but' about it. Just do it. Where's the telephone you're using?"

"On a table near the window, sir."

"How far from the body?"

"About three yards, sir."

"Is there a newspaper in the room?"

"On this table, sir. *The Daily Sentinel*."

"I'm glad you mentioned that, Ockley. It's highly relevant. I want you to go to the body, laying sheets of your *Daily Sentinel* on the floor as you go. And walking on them. Not leaving your bootmarks all over the place."

"I understand, sir."

"I want you to feel the body. You're not too dainty to do it, are you?"

"No, sir."

"Put your hand under his shirt, the back of it against his

skin. Then come back and tell me whether it's warm or not. And Ockley!"

"Sir?"

"Remove your glove before you do it. *And . . . don't . . . touch . . . anything . . . else*. Understand?"

"Yes, sir."

After the faint thump of the receiver being laid down there was silence. Then a muffled noise and Ockley's voice again.

"Sir? It's . . . it's warm." The words came out as if forced past shaking lips.

Inkbarrow pulled a face. What kind of a puling milksop was Ockley that he couldn't touch a dead man's chest without queasiness. "You didn't like that, did you, Ockley?" he said derisively.

"No, sir." He spoke in a whisper, the words just making it across the expanse of dark moor. But for Inkbarrow they contained in them undertones of the accusation, *Sadistic bastard*! And, perversely, it didn't displease him. The lad had to learn sometime. He couldn't be wetnursed all his service. "For God's sake pull yourself together, Ockley," he snapped. "Is there anything else of significance in the room?"

"I don't think so, sir."

"You've looked? Properly?"

"Yes, sir. I'm looking now."

"H'm. Is there anyone else living in the house?" He snorted more Brown Rappee up his nose, anaesthetizing his sinuses.

"No, sir. His housekeeper's snowed in at the other end of the village."

"Who found him then?"

"Mr Ogmore, the vicar, sir. At about eight-thirty. Then he came for me. He said he'd invited the doctor over for dinner. When he didn't arrive and he couldn't get an answer by telephoning him, he came across the churchyard to look for him. It's only fifty yards or so. . . ."

"Door unlocked?"

"Yes, sir. Mr Ogmore knocked several times and waited. When he didn't get an answer he opened the door and called out. Then he walked in. He was very shaken, sir."

"What was he wearing?"

There was a short silence. "Wearing, sir? The vicar?"

"The vicar, Ockley. Who else?"

"Er, well, sir, an overcoat of course. And a hat . . ." He trailed off uncertainly.

"You forgot his dog-collar and silk dicky, Ockley." Inkbarrow was at his most sardonic. "Being January with snow up to his armpits, I'll accept he would be wearing a coat and hat. What about his footwear?"

"I . . . I'm afraid I didn't notice, sir."

"But he walked in the murder room, Ockley. Haven't you anticipated what footmarks we need to eliminate?" His voice sharpened. "There *are* footmarks, aren't there? I haven't made you waste a *Daily Sentinel* for nothing?"

He heard the Adam's apple working. "No, sir. There are wet marks on the floor and carpet. But . . . but I don't think they'll be identifiable, sir."

"I see. Well, we'd better explain that to the Director of the Forensic Science Laboratories, hadn't we, Ockley? We wouldn't want him to waste the time of his trained staff when P.C. Ockley has given his opinion on a subject in which he is so self-evidently an expert." He paused a moment, gathering together his anger to fling at the luckless constable. "I've been very patient with your thick-headedness, Ockley," he rasped, "and your downright inefficiency. You and I will have an accounting when I get there. You understand?"

"Sir, I only . . ."

"Don't answer me back." He swallowed his anger but the acid of his displeasure remained. "Where is the vicar now?"

"He returned to the vicarage . . . I think, sir."

"You think? Ockley, please don't think so much. Be *positive*, man. Anyway, I'll talk to him when I arrive. You said Roath's housekeeper was cut off by the snow. What's the position where you are?"

"Well, sir, we can only move around the perimeter of the common here. We've shovelled the paths clear for walking."

"Who's 'we', Ockley?"

"Well, all of us this end of the village, sir."

Inkbarrow felt himself to be superlatively patient. "All right," he said indulgently, "who are 'all of us'?"

"The vicar, sir. Doctor Roath, of course. The Bungays next door to him. Lieutenant-Colonel Tysoe at the far end. Mr Ryan at The Red Cow. And me. None of us can reach the rest of the village. . . ."

A car pulled into the drive of Inkbarrow's house, its main beams sweeping light and shadows across the glass of the door. "Just a minute," he said, "I've a caller."

He unlatched the door to the constable driver. His cap and the shoulders of his coat were spotted with white. He brought cold air in with him. He saluted, shaking snow on to the floor. "Inspector Walton says everybody's been informed, sir, and the back-up teams are standing by for instructions. He reports that the road's still blocked."

Inkbarrow told him to wait. To Ockley, he said, "This commonland of yours. When it's not covered in snow, what is it?"

"Just grass, sir."

"It's level? No trees or other obstacles?"

"No, sir."

"A helicopter could land on it?"

"I suppose so, sir." He didn't sound too certain. But then, Inkbarrow thought with resignation, Ockley wasn't certain about anything.

He gave instructions to the driver to contact the Chief Superintendent, Administration. He required the use of a helicopter equipped for night landings. And he wanted it straight away with the pilot fully briefed on the location and topography of Upper Howick. When the driver had returned to his car, Inkbarrow spoke to Ockley. "You can't help about the actual murder, I suppose?" He muttered, "I should be so lucky."

"No, sir."

"Well, Ockley, it's obviously a local job. Somebody from one of the places you've just mentioned."

"It seems so, sir."

"No suggestions for a suspect?"

"No, sir." The resentment and withdrawal were still there.

"Or for a motive?" Jesus, he thought, it's like talking to a dummy.

"No, sir."

Inkbarrow sighed. "Please don't be sullen, Ockley. You make things very difficult. Suppose you start by telling me what *you* know of Roath. A sort of mini-biography."

There was silence, then Ockley said, "Excuse me, sir, may I smoke?"

"No you bloody well can't! You're not suggesting you should litter the place with matchsticks and ash and cigarette butts, are you? Not on top of what you've already done?"

"I'm sorry, sir. Of course not."

"Doctor Roath, Ockley. Start with his age and so-on. I know him only by repute."

"Well, sir, he's about thirty-five and he's been here two years. He's unmarried and lives on his own. Mrs Rogers is his housekeeper. He drives a green Austin thirteen-hundred, sir, and spends a lot of time in town . . . clubs and that sort of thing. . . ."

"Do you know anything of his reputation, Ockley?"

"You mean as a doctor, sir?"

"No I don't mean as a doctor. I mean as a woman-chaser."

"Only that he does go out with them, sir."

"H'm. It seems, Ockley, that I know more about his activities than you do."

"Yes, sir. He doesn't spend much time here; only attends surgery and makes a few calls. . . ."

"His surgery, Ockley. You've checked it of course?"

"No, sir. I've been . . ."

"Oh, for God's sake, Ockley! Do it straight away. For all you know our murderer may be hiding in the house. And check for any drugs in the medicine cabinet. See if there are any missing. That's something else you should have considered."

"Yes, sir."

"And Ockley!"

"Sir?"

"Don't touch anything or let that bloody dog back in."

"No, sir."

"Ockley!"

"Sir?"

"Get a jerk into it, will you."

While he waited Inkbarrow finished the gin and tonic, his forefinger tapping impatiently against the door glass. The hand holding the receiver was chilled. The central heating was acting up again. So was his stomach, trying to digest the pre-cooked dinner he had eaten earlier. He balanced Brown Rappee on a thumbnail, then vacuumed it up his nostrils. His eyes watered but his respiratory system made no other protest.

"Sir?" Ockley had been hurrying. Inkbarrow could hear his heavy breathing. "Couldn't find the way to it at first, sir. Not from inside."

"The cabinet, Ockley."

"It's unlocked, sir. I can't really say if anybody's been to it. It's difficult to tell whether stuff has been taken. . . ."

"The good Lord save me from C.I.D. rejects," Inkbarrow muttered to himself. "All right," he said aloud. "Let's get back to the mini-biographies. The vicar next."

"Mr Ogmore, sir. He lives with Mrs Ogmore at the vicarage. He's been here a long time and is fairly elderly. I don't think he would do it."

"No, I wouldn't think so either," Inkbarrow said witheringly. "But we'll keep an open mind about it, shall we? A clerical dog-collar doesn't give him automatic absolution. The other man you mentioned; the colonel type. Tell me about him."

"Lieutenant-Colonel Tysoe, sir. He's retired Royal Artillery and keeps horses."

"Why don't I know him?"

"He hasn't been here long, sir." Ockley paused and only the hissing of static could be heard. "Sir, he's quarrelled with Doctor Roath."

"Knowing Roath, I shouldn't think that difficult. What about?"

"Over the colonel's horses, sir. He grazes them on the common. One of them pulled its tether and got into Doctor Roath's garden. It trampled things about and caused a fair bit of damage. So he had this quarrel with Colonel Tysoe. . . ."

"Well? Did they slap one another's wrists? For God's sake, Ockley, tell me details. Not have me drag them from you."

"Colonel Tysoe's a very excitable gentleman, sir, when he gets annoyed. He has a very quick temper. I'm sure," he added hastily, "it doesn't really amount to anything serious."

"I'm glad he takes you into his confidence, Ockley. How old is he?"

"In his sixties, sir."

"Description?"

"Thin and wiry, sir, with white hair and moustache. He limps a bit and uses a walking stick."

"But active? Riding his horses?"

"Not really, sir. They're pretty old. He just keeps them. . . ."

"I'll come back to him. Go on with the next."

The Bungays, sir. The old man and his wife are decent respectable people. The daughter isn't too bad either. But hippie like her brother, Charlie. He's her twin, sir; staying with them, although he's usually in London. He's got long hair and a coat down to his ankles . . ."

"I know the type, Ockley. Workshy, scruffy bastards to a man. She's pretty?"

"Kathleen, sir?"

"If she's his sister, yes."

"She is, sir."

"What's the boy doing in Upper Howick apart from living with his parents?"

"He's not working, sir. Most of the time he's in the Red Cow with one or other of the village girls."

"Who did you say runs the Red Cow?"

"Mr Ryan, sir."

"So? Elaborate, Ockley. You're not sending out telegrams."

"He drinks a lot, sir. His wife does most of the serving behind the bar. She's his second wife, sir, and used to be the barmaid there. She's very much younger than he is. He breeds Jack Russell terriers."

"That's not a crime, Ockley. Although not the sort of dogs you go in for, eh?"

Ockley's alsatian had flunked the requirements for use as a

police dog and had been taken over by the constable to save it from destruction. Inkbarrow thought they made a well matched pair. "And what about you?" he asked.

"Me, sir?"

"Yes, you. What were you doing when all this was going on in your village? The patch you're responsible for: paid to look after." He pinched snuff into his nose, sniffing it up irritably.

"I was on patrol, sir," he said defensively. "From about seven to eight."

Ockley's being on duty didn't surprise Inkbarrow. Giving him his due, he was exactly the type of bloody fool to conscientiously patrol a dark and deserted snowbound village. "What did you see?" he asked.

"Nothing really, sir. Only that Doctor Roath's lights were on."

"Which meant something?"

"Not really, sir. The same lights were on when Mr Ogmore called me and I came here."

"No surgery this evening?"

"I don't think so, sir. I would have noticed the outside light."

"You saw no one?"

"I saw Doctor Roath earlier, sir. At about six o'clock."

Inkbarrow waited. When nothing came he snapped, "Well, come on, Ockley. Where did you see him? What was he doing? Standing on his bloody head?"

"Sir. He . . . he was talking to Kathleen Bungay at his gate. I saw them when I was getting some coal in."

"You're sure?"

"Well, it was dark, sir, and some distance away. Doctor Roath seemed upset . . . annoyed."

"And the girl?"

"I don't know, sir. Her back was towards me."

"What happened then?"

"I don't know, sir. I didn't wait to see."

"You don't damned well know anything, Ockley, do you?" There was no answer to this. "Right, Ockley, how long is the cord on the telephone you're holding?"

"About two yards, sir."

"Can you reach the body holding the telephone?"

"Yes, sir."

"Do it then." He waited, hearing the sounds of Ockley's moving. "You're still listening?"

Ockley swallowed audibly. "Yes, sir."

"Right. You know I shall be there very soon?"

"Yes, sir."

"You know that I'll be followed by the pathologist? By the laboratory searchers?"

"Yes, sir."

"So you appreciate it's important to describe everything you see? Accurately; not missing a single detail. You understand?"

"Yes, sir."

"Describe the head injuries to me. First of all their location. And Ockley!"

"Sir?"

"Try not to puke up until you're out of the room."

"No, sir." Inkbarrow could hear Ockley's uneven breathing as he studied the dead man's head. "Sir, there are three lacerated gashes on the right temple, each about an inch to an inch and a half long. The . . . the skull is showing beneath two of them. One of them has . . ."—Ockley gulped—". . . has brain coming from it."

There was a silence for a few moments and Inkbarrow said impatiently, "Get on with it, Ockley. Time's getting short."

"There's a split over the left cheekbone, sir . . . the mouth . . . the lips are torn badly. That's where the blood's been coming from. I can't see how many teeth are missing, sir, but there are three . . . no, four . . . near him. They're broken . . ." His voice faded and there was hard breathing as if he were about to vomit.

"Ockley!"

"Sir?" The word was the ghost of an echo, hardly a whisper.

Inkbarrow spoke sternly. "Pull yourself together, Ockley, and don't act like an old woman. You're a two-thousand pounds a year police officer; equipped to deal with major calamities, civil disorders and Acts of God." And God help us, he said; almost, but not quite, under his breath. "What else is there about him? Tell me about his legs. The ones without the trousers on them, Ockley, and therefore of importance."

"There's a sort of scratch mark on one of them, sir."

"Ah! Why do I have to drag vital information out of you?"

"They aren't very noticeable, sir."

"They?"

"There are two, sir."

"All right, Ockley," Inkbarrow said wearily. "Describe them to me."

"They're about an inch apart—perhaps a little more—and both about two inches long, sir."

"Their position and direction?"

"Just above the left knee, sir, and across the leg at a slight angle."

"Bleeding?"

"No, sir."

"All right. Go back to the table, Ockley, and keep on your *Daily Sentinel*." He waited a moment or two, then asked, "You're back?"

"Yes, sir."

"Right. Now let's do a bit of theoretical detective work while we're waiting. You know we have to make guesses—inspired guesses if you like, Ockley—but guesses nevertheless?"

"I didn't know, sir."

"To suspect someone is to guess, Ockley. If you *knew*, it wouldn't be guessing would it?"

"I see what you mean, sir."

"I'm so glad. Now we have to guess, Ockley. Then add it all up and see if those hairs and fibres you and your bloody dog have been trampling into the carpeting support the guess."

The car driver knocked at the door again and Inkbarrow reached across, releasing the lock and admitting him. "Hold on," he said to Ockley.

"A message from Operations Room, sir. A helicopter will be landing on the football ground very shortly. I'm to point out, sir, that it's a Sikorsky Sioux and has room for only one passenger."

"I don't give a damn what it is," Inkbarrow grunted. "Just so long as it gets me there."

He returned to Ockley. "Right, Ockley, let's start guessing.

What about Ryan's wife? She's an ex-barmaid and probably spreads it around a bit." He smacked his lips. "And we know Roath, don't we? *Cherchez la femme*'s a good hook for a detective to hang his hat on. And a woman is as probable a reason for getting your head bashed in as any I know. Has Roath been having it off with her while her husband was playing round with his terriers?"

He heard the glop sound again. "Doctor Roath was often in the bar, sir, but I've never seen them in any circumstances that . . ."

Inkbarrow cut him short. "I didn't suppose you would, Ockley. They wouldn't be likely to do it in the middle of the common. What about Ryan? He sounds Irish to me. A man with a quick temper and a ready blow."

"I don't think he's Irish, sir."

"Well all right, how would I know? But is he the type to object to Roath's dipping into his private barrel of honey?"

"Barrel of honey? I'm sorry, sir . . ."

"If you insist on crudity, Ockley; is he the type to object to Roath's tailing his wife?"

"I see, sir. I don't honestly know he had any cause to. But I suppose he could . . ."

"You're being so helpful, Ockley. Let's assume he did. So what did he do it with, eh? A bungstarter? A beer bottle? Only if he did, it would have been premeditated wouldn't it? Walking across the common carrying a weapon for anyone to see."

"It seems so, sir."

Inkbarrow sighed audibly. "Let's consider this hippie-type character you've got hanging around the village. Benfield or whatever his name is."

"Bungay, sir."

"It doesn't matter what his name is, it's a fair bet he's on drugs."

"I hadn't heard, sir. He's only been here just over a week."

"It's your village, Ockley. A small place. Not like a city. You should know everyone intimately. What they do, how they do it; even how many times a day they do it. Have you considered this Bungay lad might be running short of whatever it is he's hooked on? That Upper Howick isn't exactly the place to locate a pusher?"

"It would be unlikely, sir," he admitted cautiously.

"Of course it would! And where better to find narcotics than in a doctor's surgery? Had you thought of that?"

"It hadn't occurred to me, sir."

"Well, has it occurred to vou that it might have been him you saw having words with Roath at six o'clock? And not his sister?"

Inkbarrow could fancy he heard the thought strike Ockley. "It . . . it couldn't have been, sir."

"No? Tell me why not. You saw her face?"

"Not really, sir. It was dark. But her hair . . ."

"Go on." In the silence that followed he waited for the realisation that should ignite even Ockley's gelid brain.

"I . . . I see what you mean, sir. I just didn't think."

"I can't imagine you did. So? Could it have been?"

"Yes, sir," he admitted reluctantly.

"Never be afraid to admit you can be wrong, Ockley. So we could justifiably guess that Bungay, snowed up in a Godforsaken backwoods, runs out of whatever it is he shoves into himself and has a stab at stealing a substitute from Roath's surgery. Roath catches him in the act—he's probably already refused to supply him and they've quarrelled—and Bungay kills him. You think that's a fair summary?"

"I think it could be. sir."

"Well, I don't," Inkbarrow snapped. "It answers none of the questions that follow. Like, why did he remove Roath's trousers? And why wasn't he found dead in the surgery? And what weapon did Bungay do it with? Back to our problem of the weapon, Ockley, eh?"

"Yes, sir."

"You don't think Roath could have been messing around with Bungay's sister?"

Ockley made a helpless sound. "I hadn't *heard*, sir."

"A few words with her, Ockley, and we'd soon know wouldn't we? But I'm not there to ask her so I have to rely on your local knowledge. Such as it is. You appreciate how important you are to me at this moment, Ockley?"

"Yes, sir, and I'm certainly trying to be helpful."

Inkbarrow grimaced at his reflection. *Yes, sir; no, sir.* He could guess what Ockley was calling him in his pallid little mind. "Black Jack" Inkbarrow. He'd heard from one of his better lads that they called him that behind his back. And he was proud of the name. He'd earned it. It was good for discipline that he should be feared. And respected. And, by God, he'd earned that too. He hadn't missed out on a murder yet; never needing to call in Scotland Yard.

"Be helpful about this Colonel Tysoe man, Ockley. You haven't told me very much about him. He lives on his own?"

"No, sir. There's a Mrs Tysoe. And he has a man called Scully who does gardening for him and looks after the horses."

"You didn't tell me about Scully, Ockley."

"No, sir. He lives at the other end of the village. I thought . . ."

"And you thought right, Ockley. So why bring him into it at all? My time's too valuable to be wasted on people who can't be connected. I don't suppose he *can* be, Ockley?"

"I wouldn't think so, sir. We're completely cut off from his end by deep drifts. Nobody could walk in."

"What about the colonel? You remarked he had a quick temper."

"Yes, sir. But I'm sure only when provoked. I've always thought him a nice enough . . ."

"Ockley! You seem to possess a very milk-and-water attitude to your fellowmen. To be a good policeman, lad, you have to assume everyone's a villain. And they usually are in one respect or another."

"I'll try and remember that, sir."

"You'll shape up better if you do. So what provoked our saintly colonel to violence with Roath?"

"Doctor Roath found one of the colonel's horses in his garden, sir, and started hitting at it with a rake-handle. Colonel Tysoe heard the horse neighing and came out. When he saw what was happening he . . . I believe he hit Doctor Roath with his stick . . ."

"Ah! We're getting to the nub at last, Ockley. What sort of stick?"

"I don't actually know, sir. A walking stick, I think."

"Why don't you know? Haven't you done anything about it?"

"Not really, sir. Doctor Roath didn't wish to press a charge . . ."

Inkbarrow glared at the mouthpiece of his receiver. "Ockley! You are a bloody fool and very close to being put on a charge of neglecting your duty. An assault is an assault whichever way you look at it. And what about the offence of permitting a horse to stray? And a Breach of the Peace? Not forgetting cruelty to an animal, eh? I assume you neglected to interview either party and take statements for the information of your Divisional Chief Superintendent?"

"Not neglected, sir. I made a note in my Station Occurrence Book . . ."

"Which is a magnificent achievement, Ockley, and should get you on the short list for the Queen's Police Medal."

"Sir, it didn't seem worth pursuing something that had finish . . ."

"Roath's finished, Ockley. Are you still of the same opinion about your colonel?"

There was no answer although Inkbarrow could hear Ockley's agitated breathing. The lad was softer than he had ever imagined.

"Ockley! Answer me! There is such a thing as dumb insolence, you know."

"Yes, sir." His voice was a breath above a whisper. "I'm sorry. I didn't think. I'm not really myself tonight . . ."

"I'll accept that, Ockley. How long ago was this trouble between them?"

"Three days, sir. Just before the snow started."

"Three days of sitting on your backside doing nothing, eh? Do you think Colonel Tysoe could have done it with a walking stick, Ockley?"

"No, sir . . . the wounds . . . not really, sir."

"That's the first sensible conclusion you've arrived at. Nor do I. So we're not left with much are we, Ockley?"

The driver was knuckling the glass of the door and Inkbarrow opened it. "The helicopter's just landing, sir."

"Right. Tell Operations Room I'm on my way." He returned to the telephone. "Ockley!"

"Sir?"

"Get what car lights you can shining on the common. I'll be with you in a few minutes."

"Sir . . . before you come . . . I think you should listen to me . . ."

"No, Ockley. I've done all the listening I'm going to. Now it's a time for doing things."

The helicopter shuddered in the wind gusting over the moor. The fishbowl cabin in which Inkbarrow had strapped himself was dark and cold. The flailing blades over his head lashed a black sky into a whirling turbulence of snowflakes. The pilot concentrated on maintaining height and course, a dim red glow the only interior illumination he permitted himself. Inkbarrow peered down at the shadowed whiteness, trying to identify the hummocked irregularities of the village, then seeing below parallel beams of orange light. He touched the pilot's arm and pointed. "You're overshooting," he shouted into the microphone against the racketing-noise of the engine. The pilot nodded, acknowledging the gratuitous and unwanted information and putting the helicopter into hover. He thumbed a lever and beamed a brilliant swathe of light from the belly of the aircraft on to the snow beneath. Nose-downwards, they could see the cars facing each other across a rectangle of smooth flat snow. The pilot turned down the corners of his mouth and did things with both the lever between his knees and that by his side.

Hovering a yard above the ground and sending up a whirlwind of snow, he held the helicopter steady against the drifting wind. He shook his head at Inkbarrow. "I can't land," he said into his microphone. "Looks too deep. You'll have to jump. Can you do?"

Inkbarrow looked down. He could see Ockley struggling waist-deep through the snow towards them. He nodded impatiently, pulling off his earphones and unbuckling the harness.

Ockley helped him to his feet with one hand, holding his helmet steady against the downdraught of the spinning blades with the other. They both floundered through the clogging snow to the perimeter of the common. There were two other men watching by thir cars. Inkbarrow ignored them.

He followed Ockley into the tiny office attached to his house. He stamped snow from his boots on to the polished linoleum and said, "Well, Ockley?"

Ockley was pale and still breathing hard from his exertions in the snow. "Sir?"

"We know who killed Roath, don't we?" His eyes never left those of the constable. When he didn't reply, he said, "Was it about your wife?"

The constable nodded dumbly.

"And you quarrelled over her?"

He nodded again. "I found some letters. He'd been . . . he'd been . . ." He stopped and tears suddenly brimmed in his eyes. "And he was her doctor."

"She's here?"

"No, sir. At her mother's. That's when I found the letters. I telephoned her and she told me she's . . . she's not coming back, sir."

"You had your dog with you." It was a statement not a question.

"Yes, sir." His eyes were fixed on Inkbarrow; a rabbit facing a deadly stoat.

"And it joined in the fight; attacking Roath and tearing his trousers? Scratching his leg with its teeth?"

"Yes, sir. He's a good dog, sir. He was only helping me . . ."

"And you aren't so stupid as you've been trying to convince me are you, Ockley." His voice was harsh, forbidding. "You actually profited from your little tour with the Department. You remembered about the identification of animal hairs and saliva. You *had* to burn the trousers. You *had* to take your dog in on the second visit. *And* let me know you'd done so in case its hairs were found in the room." He smiled grimly at the white-faced Ockley. "And who else but a policeman, Ockley, carries his own weapon around with him without question? The most efficient and murderous weapon of them all in the wrong hands. *Lignum vitae* with a solid core of lead. Innocent, silent and terribly certain, Ockley, eh? But very, very identifiable and impossible to leave behind." He snapped finger and thumb imperatively. "Your truncheon, Ockley. Give it to me."

The constable, his eyes still fastened hypnotically on Inkbarrow, hooked his thumb in the leather loop and pulled it slowly from the special pocket in his trousers.

Inkbarrow held out his hand. "You fool, Ock . . ."

He never finished the sentence for Ockley suddenly yelled, "SHE TOLD ME! YOU TOO . . .!", not stopping his flailing until the Chief Superintendent's head was a bone-splintered pulp bleeding on to the polished linoleum.

". . . SIR!"